"NO, CATHY?" JACK WHISPERED AGAINST HER mouth "You don't want this?"

Her eyes opened slowly. "What?" she murmured.

"This," he said, bending to her again. "Me kissing you. Holding you." He trailed his lips along the line of her jaw to her ear. "Touching you. With my hands, with my mouth. Do you want that, *querida*? Do you want me to do that, Cathy?"

His deep blue eyes held an intensity that made her breath catch and her knees grow weak. She realized with a shiver of emotion that his hands, threaded into her hair and cradling the back of her head, were trembling.

He wanted her. Wanted her so much he was trembling.

"Say it, Cathy," Jack urged her. "Tell me."

His lips against her skin, his breath on her cheek stirred sensations as lush as the tropical forest after a rain. She threaded her own hands into his gold-tipped hair, clasping him with insistence and demand that equaled his. "Touch me," she pleaded, her voice low and breathy and as sensual as the jungle around them. "I want you to. I want you to touch me. Do it. . . ."

WHAT ARE *LOVESWEPT* ROMANCES?

They are stories of true romance and touching emotion. We believe those two very important ingredients are constants in our highly sensual and very believable stories in the LOVESWEPT *line. Our goal is to give you, the reader, stories of consistently high quality that may sometimes make you laugh, sometimes make you cry, but are always fresh and creative and contain many delightful surprises within their pages.*

Most romance fans read an enormous number of books. Those they truly love, they keep. Others may be traded with friends and soon forgotten. We hope that each LOVESWEPT *romance will be a treasure—a "keeper." We will always try to publish*

LOVE STORIES YOU'LL NEVER FORGET
BY AUTHORS YOU'LL ALWAYS REMEMBER

The Editors

DOWN AND DIRTY

LINDA WARREN

BANTAM BOOKS
NEW YORK • TORONTO • LONDON • SYDNEY • AUCKLAND

DOWN AND DIRTY

A Bantam Book / July 1994

ISBN 0-553-44403-4

Published simultaneously in the United States and Canada

Bantam Books are published by Bantam Books, a division of Bantam Doubleday Dell Publishing Group, Inc. Its trademark, consisting of the words "Bantam Books" and the portrayal of a rooster, is Registered in U.S. Patent and Trademark Office and in other countries. Marca Registrada. Bantam Books, 1540 Broadway, New York, New York 10036.

PRINTED IN THE UNITED STATES OF AMERICA

OPM 0 9 8 7 6 5 4 3 2 1

ONE

A mariachi band was playing passably in the corner of the dim, noisy, crowded cantina. Mexican beer was flowing in abundance at the bar. But neither the *cerveza* nor the music was the center of anyone's attention. La Stela was the kind of place where a man came looking for a woman—or something equally dangerous.

Jack Gibraltar found her on his third sweep of the bar, just before he'd decided to drain his beer and leave, and the shock of recognition knocked him back on his blithe assumptions like a hit of tequila.

What the hell had she done to herself?

Her dark hair was loose, sexy, and disheveled. The neckline of her embroidered Mexican blouse had slipped down over one fair-skinned shoulder, and her long suede skirt rode low on her hips, as if she'd deliberately left a couple of buttons undone.

Maybe she had, Jack realized as masculine appreciation rippled along every nerve in his body. The clinging skirt, which outlined the curve of her backside, looked as if one deliberate, sexy movement would send it shimmying down over her hips. And she looked, for God's sake, capable of it.

Jack made a sound in the back of his throat, a sound that was shaded with ideas he'd had no intention of having when he went there, looking for her.

One of the men lounging at the bar beside him glanced toward him, then followed his gaze, peering around one of the stone pillars of La Stela's fake–pre-Columbian decor. The man let out a low chuckle and grinned back at Jack. "*La gringa?*" He gave her another once-over, his eyes narrowed in speculation, then raised his eyebrows. "*Simpática*. She's new here, eh?"

Jack swore silently. She was new here, all right. A couple of hours ago she'd been staring him down through horn-rimmed glasses, her briefcase clutched deftly under one elbow as she waved her archaeology lecture notes in front of his face and demanded access to his computer files. She wanted, she claimed, to clear her aunt's name, and she fully expected Jack to help her do it. A Woman With a Cause, if he'd ever met one.

Which he had.

He'd reacted in the only way that made sense under the circumstances. He'd shut the door in her face. Who the hell would have thought she'd actually show up at this place, slugging back her drink as if it were ginger ale, dressed like . . .

Her aunt. Jack clenched his jaw and cursed the insight. Clearly she had borrowed the clothes. The archaeology professor in the linen suit couldn't own anything like this outfit. She must have a key to her aunt's apartment, and she must have helped herself to the contents of the closet. On Madrid's matronly figure, the Mexican blouse and skirt would have looked merely comfortable. On her niece, the effect was . . . trouble looking for a place to happen.

In this place he'd give her five minutes, tops, before she was in it up to her off-the-shoulder neckline. Jack shut his eyes, willing the image of the woman out of his consciousness. He didn't need any more trouble than he already had. He wasn't looking for the kind you got from women. Especially not from a woman on a damned crusade. That was why he'd sent her packing.

For an acutely uncomfortable moment he wondered what else Madrid might have left lying around for her niece to find. A couple of the possibilities snapped at him like the frayed ends of a hangman's noose.

The man beside him was glancing questioningly from Jack to the woman, trying to determine if Jack had a claim.

Jack returned his glance, jaw set, but male rivalry wasn't what tightened his fist on his mug. Jack didn't have any claim. What Jack Gibraltar had was a problem.

Swearing again, Jack picked up his beer and wove his way through the crowd. Half the *cerveza* had been jostled out of his mug by the time he got across the room, but there was enough left to slosh out over the rim when he smacked it down on the bar. She turned toward the sound, startled.

Jack gave her the kind of smile that passed for friendly concern in La Stela. "What the *hell*," he inquired politely, "do you think you're doing here?"

Catherine Moore took in his presence, her

eyes widening at the first sight she'd had of him since he'd refused to let her into his apartment. Black leather jacket, jeans, don't-be-cruel deep blue eyes fringed by thick lashes, long sun-streaked hair, a mouth made for irony and exit lines. The one he'd given her about taking herself back to the library had rolled off his tongue like music, punctuated by the sound of the door slamming in her face.

She hadn't even considered heeding the advice. The kind of answers she was looking for weren't going to be found in a library. But a thought dawned on her now as she stared back at the man in front of her, his solid, lean frame supported by one elbow on the bar, his attitude hooked over his shoulder just like his black leather jacket. She hadn't merely stepped out of the library when she'd walked into La Stela. She'd stepped across the line into Jack Gibraltar's territory. And he wasn't a man who tolerated trespassers.

A shiver ran down Catherine's spine like the touch of a fingertip. Swallowing, she tightened her fingers around her glass, let out a long, barely perceptible breath, and answered his question. "You know what I'm doing here," she said, the words not quite steady. "You told me to go ahead and try."

Jack Gibraltar's mouth quirked up at one corner. The smile would have been charming if he hadn't been looking at her as if she'd just raised the stakes and he was holding all the aces. Catherine straightened her shoulders defensively. Her aunt's blouse slipped a little farther down her arm, and his eyes followed it in a slow, contemplative appraisal that brought heat rushing to the surface of her skin.

His gaze followed the flush that rose from her bare shoulders to her face. "I didn't think you'd do it," he said finally.

"Why not?" she challenged him.

"Because you don't look stupid, *Professor*."

Catherine made herself hold his gaze without blinking. She knew she wasn't stupid. She was smart enough to realize, for instance, that intelligence was beside the point.

"Listen, lady," he said when she didn't speak again. "Maybe I told you to go ahead and find your own answers to your aunt's problems, but this is not a place you casually wander into one night when you have nothing better to occupy your time."

No, it wasn't. But she hadn't casually wandered in there. And she wasn't going to casually wander out either. Not without some answers.

She gave herself a moment to gaze into her drink, working up her nerve, then lifted the glass and took another hefty slug. "My aunt used to wander in here quite a lot, didn't she?"

Disbelief flashed across his face. "Yeah, your aunt used to wander in here. And do you need someone to remind you what happened to her?"

"No. I don't."

He gave her a look that was meant to end the discussion with universal agreement of his point, and, no doubt, send her back to the library, where he thought she belonged.

Catherine's temper flickered, then sparked. "I know quite well what happened to her. She lost her job, her reputation, her place in an academic community—all over a scandal that was . . . a mistake. My aunt—" She broke off, then curled her hand into a fist. "My aunt was not involved in forging a Mayan artifact and trying to pass it off as authentic in a shady deal to a private collector!"

One of Jack Gibraltar's eyebrows rose in disdain.

Catherine's anger flared in reaction. "She had to leave her place at the university. Now she's in forced exile somewhere because not one of her former colleagues will have anything to do with her. I want to clear her name once and for all, Mr. Gibraltar. And I intend to do it!"

He studied her a moment, his expression skeptical. "Why?"

"Because—" She stopped, out of words after her uncharacteristic outburst. She hadn't expected him to ask why. Two reasons breezed into her mind: Madrid had started her on the road toward a Ph.D. in archaeology and had stood in for Catherine's mother after she had died. Jack Gibraltar, she assumed, knew all that. But none of it explained what Catherine Moore was doing in a Chetumal bar, trying her best to consort with smugglers, con artists, and the likes of Jack Gibraltar. What had brought her there was a small, niggling, unbearably painful doubt that she'd choke on before she'd admit it to anyone. She had to prove her aunt's innocence because she herself wasn't sure of it.

Jack Gibraltar raised his mug, drained it in one long swallow, then put it down on the bar, his gaze on Catherine's face. Slowly, his mouth curved in a faint, unreadable smile.

Catherine felt a wave of reaction chase up her spine to her throat. She swallowed hard and shut her eyes for a moment, trying to ignore the man in front of her. Her library-trained brain provided a slew of adjectives to describe him: dictatorial, arrogant, virile, dangerous. The adjectives won. When she glanced at him again, she felt another shiver travel up her spine.

"She's my aunt, Mr. Gibraltar. Shall we just leave it at that?"

"Leaving it at that's fine with me. You're the one who's on a *crusade*."

He made the word sound like profanity.

"Don't you have a job of your own to worry about, lady?"

"I'm on sabbatical. If I want to do some independent research, I'm free to do it."

"Independent research?"

He was mocking her, and Catherine made herself hold her ground. She'd be damned if she'd give him some weak excuse merely because he was probably going to scoff at the truth. "I thought if I put in an appearance here, wearing my aunt's clothes, one of her former . . . colleagues . . . might show an interest in whatever she was involved in before she left her job."

He processed that without noticeable incredulity—though he must have had some, she admitted honestly. Madrid had made a habit of circumventing the potential damage done by artifact looters by dealing with them directly. It was risky business even for Madrid. The idea that Catherine could pull it off was hardly worth considering.

"Any takers?" he asked her.

She shrugged again. "Just you."

He peered at her and said, "Listen, you hang out here, acting like you've got something to sell, you'd better be prepared to deliver on your promises."

She took a deep breath before she answered him. "I always deliver on my promises."

Five seconds of silence followed, then he said, "Well. Maybe you are in the right place." His eyes slid down over her blouse, then met hers with the kind of insinuation that couldn't be mistaken.

Catherine hadn't completely lost her temper since the university library had misshelved her thesis. She wasn't, she told herself, going to lose it over the impudent suggestions of a lean, sun-bronzed, blue-eyed American who was a little too confident of his south-of-the-border turf.

"This wasn't my first choice," she said almost evenly. "But since you refused to help me—"

"I *refused* to let some unauthorized, unintroduced archaeologist go tiptoeing through my computer files, leaving a lot of messy footprints! You have a problem with that?"

"What I have is a lot of questions with no answers. And don't try to tell me you didn't know I was Madrid's niece."

"So—you have questions, ask your aunt."

"I don't know where she is!"

He stared back at her, returning her glare with enough smoldering sparks of his own to ignite the wooden bar.

"Do *you*?" Catherine asked.

Several moments passed, filled with no answers.

He glanced away from her. "Assuming I wanted to help you with your particular crusade, which, believe me, is a big assumption, just what is it you think I could do? I'm a computer hack. I wrote programs for your aunt for a few months to try to decipher a lot of funny numbers in an old Mayan book that everybody thought was worth a lot of money until the man who bought it announced it was a fake."

"And your own announcement corroborated the opinion!"

The square jaw locked. Something that

struck her as wariness hardened his blue eyes. "Just part of the job," he said tightly.

"*Just part of the job?* To make sure my aunt takes the heat for a forged Mayan codex, while you get off scot—"

"I just analyze the numbers. I don't get personally involved."

"You don't get—" She stopped herself, ignoring the blaze of anger that welled up inside her. If outrage and a sense of injustice could answer her questions, they would have been answered long ago. What she needed most, next to a few key computer files, were her wits and a cool head, and her researcher's instinct.

And that instinct told her not everything about this affair made complete sense. Including the behavior of one sunburned, insensitive expatriate who raised her temperature faster than anyone she'd ever met. She swallowed again, took a breath, and carefully loosened her fingers around her glass. "You don't get personally involved?"

He returned her level stare with unwavering resistance.

"Then . . . what are you doing here?" she said.

It was a damn good question, Jack decided sourly.

He glanced away from her, staring at one of the stone icons hanging over the bar and wondering how the hell he'd let her get around to asking it. Something about the way her throat had tightened when he'd inquired about her aunt. Something about the way she'd slipped inside his guard with her gutsy defiance and that damned outfit. And she'd latched on to just the wrong question.

He didn't have any good answers. The obvious one, that he'd suspected she just might be fool enough to turn up in La Stela, probably wouldn't convince her she ought to get her sweet little suede-covered butt out of there. Crusaders didn't usually go in for doing what was good for them on the basis of vague advice.

The complete, unvarnished truth, on the other hand, was not something Jack was inclined to share. Which left him where?

Jack dropped his gaze from the icon and covered his eyes with one hand. There wasn't any point in trying to stare down an expression that hadn't blinked in eleven hundred years. The hollow-eyed Mayan mask would win every time.

"I'm having another drink," he muttered. "You want one?"

She didn't answer. Jack reached for her glass, held it up, and pointed with his other hand for the benefit of the bartender. The man nodded, and Jack lowered the glass, stared at it, then held it to his nose and sniffed.

It *was* ginger ale. He gave Catherine another once-over, grudgingly acknowledging that she wasn't entirely lacking in common sense. She wasn't drinking herself into brainlessness. Unfortunately.

She was watching him through wide, serious brown eyes that reflected every nuance of emotion, and every flicker of too-incisive intelligence.

"Look," he offered, exasperated, when she held her silence. "I'm not the one who's responsible for your aunt quitting her job and taking off for warmer climes, okay?"

"Oh, I know. One very . . . unsatisfied . . . art collector is responsible for that."

"Yeah."

"And Mr. Blasquo won't speak to me. Or to any other archaeologist who's interested in seeing the codex."

Jack shook his head. "I don't think he's too crazy about having his name brought up in a place like this either."

"Why not?"

The bartender walked toward them with the drinks and Catherine glanced at him. Jack grinned at the man. "This is Catherine Moore," he said with exaggerated courtesy. "She's a college professor in the States. She likes to hang out in places like La Stela and she doesn't mind her name being mentioned."

The bartender shot her a skeptical glance and gave Jack an amused shrug.

"Is that supposed to embarrass me into leaving without any answers?" Catherine asked.

Jack let his mouth quirk at one corner. "I hope so."

"Actually," Catherine said, turning toward the bartender, "I'm interested in contacting a man named Blasquo. He's an art collector. I think he's been in here before."

The bartender's amused expression faded.

Jack forced himself to shrug carelessly.

When the bartender had moved off, Jack picked up his beer, studied it for a moment, then let his glance slide toward Catherine. "I'll share some ancient Mayan philosophy with you, Ms. Moore. When the gods have been relatively nice to you so far, don't ask too many questions. They just might want a human sacrifice."

"Maybe they've already had one. My aunt."

The woman ought to come with a warning label. Sexy, intelligent, persistent, and probably more dangerous than napalm.

"You knew her," she went on. "You must have known she wouldn't—"

She stopped talking abruptly and looked away from him. Then, in a gesture that reminded him of Madrid, she let go of her glass and tucked her thumbs into the waistband of her skirt. Jack felt his perceptions shift. Madrid, he realized suddenly, had been Catherine's maternal role model of a sort. The idea was a little unsettling. How much had the older woman taught her? Madrid's shrewd moves, combined with a crusader's passion, didn't bear thinking about.

Catherine glanced back at him, her gaze level, and said evenly, "I want to know what happened. Just . . . the truth."

She pulled one hand out of her waistband to tug her blouse up onto her shoulder. It gaped at the neckline in a way that was distracting as hell. Just what he needed: cleavage and a quest for The Truth.

"Sometimes," he muttered, "the truth's a little tough to take, Professor. Ask your aunt when she gets back."

She was silent for a moment, then said, "It seems to me that in this case there weren't quite enough tough breaks to go around."

He frowned at her.

"You didn't get one, for instance. You just calmly announced, after my aunt left, that your data corroborated the theory that the codex was forged."

"I just stated that the numbers we were coming up with on the codex didn't conform to any known periodicity indices such as the Mayan astronomers might have used for—"

"I know what you said! I also know you didn't bother to say it until after my aunt had already left, and no one knew how to contact her to ask her what *she* could say to defend herself!"

It was entirely possible, Jack reflected grimly, for an idealist to be too perceptive for her own good. He ran a hand through his hair, raking it back off his face, considering possible answers and what effect they'd have on Catherine Moore and her demand for The Truth. He settled on a piece of it that he figured needed reinforcing. "Look, lady. You've got me on some kind of a shortlist of volunteers to be the next human sacrifice. And you can just take me off. I'm not the victim for the job."

"And who is?" she demanded. "Who's the next human sacrifice?"

He tipped back his head and gave her a slow perusal. "I don't know, *querida*. You're the one who's dressed for it though."

She didn't respond immediately, but a spark of reaction flickered in her eyes that made Jack's blood pressure rise a few notches. Unexpected awareness jolted through him like electricity.

Jack stared at her, holding her shocked gaze with a challenge he knew damn well he should drop. She wasn't the kind of woman who would back off from the truth. And God knew there were some truths he damn well couldn't afford to have her explore.

But for reasons he didn't want to analyze, he let this one stand for a taut moment, until she drew in a sharp breath and glanced down, then looked up again.

"I'm . . . dressed for . . . camouflage," she said with more self-consciousness than she'd shown since he'd caught sight of her at the bar.

"*Camouflage?*" Jack let out a disbelieving huff of breath. "If that's all you've got to sell, Professor, I'd suggest you take it back to your hotel room and lock it up before it gets arrested for juvenile delinquency."

Her chin snapped up. "How do you know I'm selling?" she said in a tone that suddenly matched his challenge for challenge. "Maybe I'm buying."

The answer brought him up short. It had just enough nerve to shock him. Just enough promise to hold his interest. Just enough appeal to tie him in knots. Jack felt it a little too viscerally, all the way down to his private fantasies. What Catherine Moore really wanted—the stark truth—would tie him in knots all right.

This encounter was out of hand.

He set his beer down precisely on the bar, let go of the mug, and pushed his hands into his pockets. It was time to make a phone call.

To someone who didn't have to look at the way that damn neckline plunged.

To someone who'd set this operation up without taking into account one damn persistent, inconveniently idealistic, overly intelligent niece.

Something for damn sure had to be done before Catherine Moore came riding in on her Quest for The Truth and trampled all over a perfectly workable con game.

TWO

Catherine stared at the back of Jack's head, feeling her anger fade into a dawning, unwelcome realization of just how badly she had handled the encounter.

As she wrapped her fingers around her glass, it occurred to her that she should have thanked him for the drink, smiled, and politely probed for more information. She should have kept her temper and held her tongue and plied him with reasonable questions until he'd been lured into giving her some honest answers.

Either that, or she should have poured his drink down the front of his pants.

That wouldn't have netted her any more information about Madrid, but it might have made up in some small measure for the way Jack Gibraltar had probably sold her aunt out in the interest of protecting his own miserable, unprincipled, culturally illiterate hide.

She took a healthy swallow of the ginger ale, wishing it were something stronger. Dammit, she *needed* his computer files. She needed to know just what they could prove. Maybe Gibraltar had wrongly interpreted the computer data.

But her dream didn't last long. She couldn't really believe Jack Gibraltar had made an error. If he'd been working with Aunt Madrid, it was a safe bet he could read a satellite scan of a Mayan site faster than his computer could spit it out. Whatever else Madrid might have compromised on, she didn't suffer fools. Jack Gibraltar might be lying, but he wasn't wrong.

So who was? Catherine brushed her hair back from her forehead in a frustrated gesture. Her aunt? Madrid Moore was a first-rate archaeologist. Unconventional, maybe, but her scholarly work couldn't be faulted. At least not until this whole scandalous arrangement had blown up in her face, leaving her in exiled disgrace.

Jack Gibraltar, of course, came out squeaky clean and insufferably smug and in sole possession of whatever knowledge his computer had to yield.

And the only thing Catherine had learned for her efforts so far was that she was capable of staring down a lean, muscled, blue-eyed con man in a Chetumal bar and implying that she was there for the purpose of buying sex.

Exasperated with herself, disgusted with the situation, and furious with Jack Gibraltar, she picked up her purse, spun away from the bar, and wove her way through the crowd toward the front door.

Outside the bar there was not a cab in sight, only a small crowd of patrons milling around on the sidewalk, smoking and laughing over jokes Catherine didn't want to hear. A single glance made her think that the smugglers among them were probably the most trustworthy of the bunch.

Muttering silent imprecations at Jack Gibraltar, whose computer files would have precluded the necessity of being there in the first place, Catherine stepped toward the curb.

"*Buenas noches*, señorita."

The gruff, low voice was close enough to her ear to make her jump. She nodded warily at a man in a Guatemalan shirt who was smiling at her and edging close.

"*Se llama* . . . Catherine Moore, no?"

She frowned at him. "*Sí.*"

"Catherine Moore." The man smiled again. "I heard you speaking to the bartender. You find La Stela interesting?"

It was impossible for her to identify his intent. Which might have been just as well, she decided, considering the setting. "Excuse me, señ—"

"I find it so myself," he interrupted. "As does Mr. Blasquo."

"Mr. Blasquo?"

"*Sí.* He is a good . . . friend. I speak to him often. We share many of the same . . . interests."

Many of the same interests? Despite the slight accent, the man spoke excellent English. She didn't think the significant pauses before the key words had anything to do with a vocabulary search. Whatever *interests* this man shared with Blasquo, he wanted Catherine to know about them. But there was something sinister about the way he went about telling her.

She considered the information, then took a deep breath and unconsciously hooked her thumbs into the waistband of her suede skirt. She had, after all, been spreading her name around La Stela. This was the sort of result she'd hoped for.

Wasn't it?

"I would like," she said carefully, "to speak to Mr. Blasquo about a subject of mutual interest. It would be worth his while. I have contacts among archaeologists in the States."

The man's expression didn't alter, but his smile underwent a subtle change that indicated something more purposeful than Catherine wanted to deal with.

"You are having difficulty finding a cab, señorita." It was not a question. "I can offer you a ride."

She tensed, glanced quickly up and down the street, then gave the man a brief forced smile while a warning vibrated in the pit of her stomach. She wasn't up on the nuances of how to conduct this kind of business, but she wasn't totally naive either. The idea of blithely driving off with a stranger who shared an interest in Mayan artifacts didn't seem like a particularly good one. "I'm sure there will be cabs," she told him. "Perhaps . . . you could have Mr. Blasquo call me?"

The man leaned toward her and spoke, close enough so that she could feel his breath on her cheek. "He would want to be sure it was worth his while," he said softly.

No doubt. Catherine pulled her thumbs

out of her waistband and tucked her hands around her shoulder bag. And no doubt Mr. Blasquo's emissary was about to suggest that he check out the information himself before he passed the message on to his "friend." She quickly went over her options. She didn't want to offend her first potential source of information, but she wasn't going to get into a car with him either.

"I'll give you my phone number," she said firmly, reaching into her shoulder bag for a card.

The man put his hand on her arm. "No need," he said smoothly. "I will give you a ride."

Catherine pulled her arm back. The fingers around her elbow barely tightened, but her uneasiness rose sharply.

"I think," the man said, "we should continue this . . . communication . . . more privately. No?"

Catherine's smile disintegrated as she shot a glance over her shoulder toward the bar, where the crowd was shifting around, making way for someone coming out. Not one pair of eyes was aimed her way. La Stela's patrons tended to mind their own business. No one was going to interfere with a "negotiation" involving a regular and an unknown *gringa* who'd been spreading her name around the bar.

She looked back at her would-be business associate. "No," she said again.

He smiled. "*Sí.*"

She'd opened her mouth, determined to scream bloody murder if that was what it took to get her message across, when Jack Gibraltar shouldered his way through the crowd at the door and crossed the sidewalk toward them in two long steps.

"Excuse me," he said in Spanish, "but the lady is already spoken for."

The man holding Catherine's arm frowned and glanced from Jack to Catherine, hesitating just long enough for Jack to take her elbow smoothly out of the man's grip and transfer it to his own. "Let's go, *querida*," he said to her.

The Chetumal patron let out a torrent of Spanish whose meaning would have been clear even if Catherine didn't speak the language.

Jack ignored the vitriolic tone and shot back a rapid-fire answer she just managed to translate. No, he explained, the lady knew nothing about Mayan artifacts or a Señor Blasquo. The man had been mistaken; the lady had no doubt thought she was discussing the decor of La Stela while she waited for Jack to pick her up for their date.

Sheer astonishment silenced Catherine completely. Still trying to figure out what in God's name was going on, she let Jack tuck her hand into the crook of his arm and walk her half a block to a stripped-down red Nissan Tracker. He put her in the car, shut the door, and nimbly hopped over the hood to get into the driver's side. He'd already pulled away from the curb before she got out her first sentence.

"Where," she asked with more composure than the situation deserved, "do you think we're going?"

He downshifted and turned a corner, then gave her a pointed glance. "*You're welcome,*" he said with sarcastic emphasis. "In case you didn't notice, I just pulled you out of a tight corner."

With a tale tall enough to make his nose grow. "All right," she granted, crossing her arms in front of her. "Thank you. But while we're noticing details, I could point out that I didn't ask for your help. And I'm not sure the corner was all that tight."

"Believe me, lady, it was plenty tight.

Your friend there didn't have your interest at heart."

"You know the man?" she asked him.

"I know what he wanted."

Catherine frowned at him, sure Jack hadn't actually heard their conversation, wondering if he'd guessed it. "What did he want?" she asked cautiously.

He looked at her, flicked his eyes down to her bare shoulder, then gave her a one-sided grin that held too much masculine sensuality. "He wanted to know your rate in pesos, *querida*. He wouldn't have been happy with a polite refusal either."

Catherine's fingers slipped off her elbows into her lap. Outrage and sheer disbelief stuck together in her throat and produced a tiny, inaudible gargle. *Her rate in pesos?*

A realization suddenly clicked: Jack Gibraltar didn't know she spoke Spanish. He'd fed some preposterous lie to her "friend" the negotiator, and now he was feeding her an even more preposterous lie, delivered in a way that clearly showed he didn't expect her to entertain a single doubt.

Catherine bristled at the insult. "What exactly was my *rate*, Mr. Gibraltar?"

He flicked another look toward her neckline. "I'm not sure," he admitted. "But I'd bet my grandmother it's more than any man can afford."

"I have a feeling you'd bet your grandmother in an all-night poker game upstairs at La Stela!"

"That's not what they do upstairs at La Stela. The kind of games that are popular involve more personal—"

"You don't have to spell it out. Though I have no doubt you're capable of it."

In her peripheral vision Gibraltar's smoldering blue eyes burned a leisurely, speculative path all along her left side, from her bare shoulder to her suede skirt, molded to her thigh by the pressure of the seat.

"Maybe I haven't spent my life in a library," he commented, drawing out the words, "but considering that I just picked you up on a street corner in a pretty questionable neighborhood, you don't have much claim to sainthood yourself."

Catherine locked her hands together in her lap. She'd be damned if she'd pull up the slipping neckline.

"Mr. Gibraltar," she said through gritted teeth, "I've already thanked you for 'rescuing' me from an unnamed danger. Could you answer my original question? Where are we going?"

"Where are you planning to go?"

"Back to my aunt's apartment."

"Alone?"

"I had hoped so. I still hope so."

This time he kept his comments to himself.

"Do you know where it is?" Catherine asked.

His muttered answer was indecipherable, but he turned at the corner in a direction that felt vaguely correct.

She studied him while he maneuvered the Tracker around the potholes of the back street they were now on, wondering whether she'd get a more satisfactory answer if she asked whether he knew where he was going.

Probably not. The man's relationship to the truth was nothing more than a passing acquaintance. If that.

He'd tell her whatever he thought was convenient for her to hear, deliver it with arrogance, and expect her powers of reason to stay on hold.

Which, she had to admit, was more or less where they'd been since she met him. *Reasonable* didn't describe her reaction to him.

He brought out aspects of her personality that would have shocked even her worldly-wise and salty-tongued Aunt Madrid.

Maybe, she reflected ruefully, that was why Madrid had barely mentioned Jack Gibraltar in their weekly phone conversations. She hadn't known how Catherine would react to a sexy, good-looking computer hack who took liberties with the truth. Or hadn't wanted to stretch the truth herself.

Catherine made herself ignore the anxiety that arose from the thought of Madrid's dealings. She knew her aunt was honest. Wasn't she? In everything that really mattered anyway. She certainly wouldn't have stretched the truth about something so important as the work she dedicated her life to.

But then, what had she been doing with the likes of Jack Gibraltar?

She shot him a glance, worriedly studying his strong profile. "How long did you work with my aunt, Mr. Gibraltar?" she ventured to ask, trying to make her voice casual.

"Long enough."

"Long enough," she repeated wryly under her breath.

"Yeah."

"You did satellite scans for the sites as well as decoding, didn't you?"

"Yeah." He added grudgingly, "I wasn't hired to do satellite scans, but she was always in too much of a hurry to wait for the archaeology department to interpret them."

Catherine turned toward him, leaning her back against the car door, propping her elbow on the back of the seat so that her straying neckline would return into place. "Was that her mistake? Being in too much of a hurry?"

He ran a hand through his hair, combing back one stray, sandy-blond lock, but didn't respond.

"Mr. Blasquo was involved in the deal from the start, wasn't he?"

"If you know all the details, why are you asking me?"

"God knows! I'm not getting very many answers."

"Maybe I don't have any. You ever consider that? I'm just a computer hack. I just do my job."

"Oh? And you just happened to come out of a shady deal looking for all the world squeaky clean and innocent."

"I *am* squeaky clean and innocent."

He said it looking her square in the eye, without even a trace of guilty hesitation.

Catherine bit her lip, feeling in spite of herself a few creeping doubts about her own accusations. She'd always thought she could recognize honesty in others.

But she'd never had an experience that quite compared with meeting Jack Gibraltar. She'd never been lied to quite so outrageously before. And the most infuriating aspect of being conned by him was that every time he gave her that exasperated, earnest look, she *wanted* to believe him, damn him!

"I'm sorry," she said firmly. "I can't buy that."

The Tracker lurched into a pothole and Catherine braced herself against the dashboard while he gave her another long appraisal. "Lady," he said, his voice a low, vibrant drawl, "the last time we got into a discussion of what you were *buying*, you ended up on a street corner with an overemotional customer."

"I ended up in a Tracker with no shock absorber and a driver who thinks speed limits apply to someone else!"

He raked a hand through his hair again in annoyance, his gaze passing over the rearview mirror. With sudden alertness he locked on to the image reflected there and muttered an oath earthy enough to defy translation.

Catherine peered over her shoulder at the white convertible behind them, frowning. "A friend of yours?" she asked.

"Not mine. Apparently your pal from the street corner didn't stay where we left him. He must have been parked in front of the bar."

Catherine squinted into the headlights. "The man who was talking to me outside the bar?"

"Yeah." He gave her a glittering blue glance. "That's one hell of a persistent customer, *querida*. What did you promise him?"

"He's not *my* customer!"

"Well, he sure as hell isn't *mine*."

"How do I know? *You're* the one who keeps bringing up the subj—" Without warning he downshifted and slid the Tracker into a side street. "What are you doing?"

"Changing direction," he said grimly. "I'll take you to my place. I'm not going to drop you off at Madrid's with our friend following you."

"Look, Mr. Gibraltar. I appreciate the caution, but I think I'd rather see it in your driving."

His mouth quirked. "Fine, then. Why don't I pull over and you can give him your address?"

"That's not necessary. I've already given it to him."

"What?"

She blinked at the shock in his voice. "I gave him my card in front of the bar. Madrid's card, actually. It has her phone number on it."

The Tracker skidded as Jack Gibraltar slammed on the brakes and Catherine snatched at the back of the seat to steady herself. When she looked up at him, he stared back at her for a second, then shut his eyes, gripped the steering wheel, and let out a long breath.

Finally he said, "I take back what I said about you not being a saint. You've gone way past crusading idealist. You're working on Joan of Arc. And we all know what happened to her."

They drove to Madrid's apartment in silence and at acceptable speeds. Their tail was nowhere in view, but since he already knew Catherine's address, there was no reason he should be, Jack figured.

This little assignment had sounded almost reasonable half an hour ago. Keep Professor Catherine Moore out of trouble and don't let anything happen to her. Piece of cake. He hadn't counted on their tag-along friend moving in on her outside the bar, but he'd figured after he extracted her from that shady artifact buyer the rest would be routine.

Wrong.

What the hell had made him think there would be anything routine about a woman who could launch a thousand fantasies?

Maybe I'm buying . . .

He slanted a glance at her as he checked the rearview mirror again. She'd fastened her seat belt and was leaning back as far as possible from the windshield. The shoulder strap crossed her chest snugly, molding the loose blouse against her breasts and revealing the fact that she wasn't wearing a bra.

That last challenging look she'd given him in the bar had held a couple of fantasies of her own. Catherine Moore had eyes that even in La Stela's dim, smoky light revealed something she wasn't quite aware she was giving away. But a man who saw that fire burning below the surface of that cool composure just might ransom his life for it. Just pack it up and cancel the insurance and hand it over as a down payment.

A minor roadblock, he'd been told over the

phone when he gave the report on Catherine. He pursed his lips in a silent whistle and uttered a few mental comments on that opinion. Ms. Moore was no minor roadblock. She was a drastic detour. Sexy, intelligent, opinionated—and worse. She was totally, uncompromisingly, unconsciously honest.

Right down to the looks she revealed in a dimly lit bar.

So what the hell was he going to do with her?

Damn good question.

He had the uneasy feeling that trying to out-logic her with a lot of conveniently unverifiable facts wasn't going to work.

He could send her off on a false trail, maybe. Or scare the pants off her.

He gritted his teeth and dismissed the images brought to his mind by that last thought.

Briefly, he considered a measure more drastic than anything that had occurred to him so far: telling her the truth.

Headlights flickered in the rearview mirror.

What was he, nuts? Tell her the truth? She couldn't even keep her phone number to herself when she was being propositioned by a two-timing, two-bit sleaze artist like the one following them now. He was going to trust her with the *truth*? It was a measure of how much she'd shaken him up that he even considered it.

No.

Not an option.

Not even a remote possibility. He was just going to have to play this the way it was shaping up: He was looking like some kind of lowlife who'd let Madrid take the rap for a mutual mistake. If Catherine Moore had him cast as the villain in a police lineup, he was just going to have to let her think he was guilty. Which shouldn't be too damn hard. She already had him *feeling* guilty, for God's sake.

He muttered an oath out loud.

Catherine Moore turned toward him, dark hair brushing across her shoulder. "What is it now?" she asked him, her eyes widening.

He let his breath out through his nose. "Nothing you want to hear," he told her.

"Try me."

Jack felt a jolt of reaction. "You know something? You ought to work on that habit you have of saying whatever comes to your mind."

She lifted her chin and leaned back against the seat. "It's worked all right for *me*."

He read the unspoken part of the sentiment without much trouble: She didn't believe he was speaking the simple truth. Hell, he wasn't even sure there was such a thing as simple truth. Certainly not in this case.

Her voice guarded, she asked, "Have you been to my aunt's apartment before?"

He had a feeling it was some kind of test. The kind that *ought* to be easy to pass.

He shrugged noncommittally. "Once or twice."

She studied him for a moment, tipping her chin at a doubtful angle, then turned back to the road as he made another turn toward Madrid's street. "No more than that?"

Jack bit back the urge to elaborate on his answer and make it more convincing. When in doubt, say nothing, he told himself. She couldn't prove him wrong.

He turned another corner, scanned the street in front of the apartment, then silently and with the resignation he was becoming accustomed to, ate his own words.

THREE

She wouldn't *have* to prove him wrong. The crowd of young boys hanging around Madrid's front lawn would do it for her. They looked up as the Tracker pulled around the corner, and broke into universal smiles as their leader, a skinny, computer-crazy kid called Ace, hopped off the bench and yelled, "Jack!"

Catherine Moore's eyebrows shot halfway up her forehead.

Luck, Jack reflected, was not running his way. He parked at the side of the street, got out of the four-wheel drive, and slammed the door.

"Jack, you would not believe what I did with my mother's computer." Ace grinned at him. "You know what you told me? About the batch files? It worked *perfectamente*, Jack. You would not believe it!"

Jack gave him a resigned grin and avoided Catherine's gaze. "Like a charm, huh?" he muttered.

"*Sí.* I did not hurt anything. She will not even know I did it."

Jack somehow doubted that, but this wasn't the time to get into the subject. "Hey, Jack," one of the other kids chimed in. "Ace wants to get a modem. He can call you up!"

Jack raised his hands and shook his head. "Yeah, well, we'll talk about that later, okay?"

"Aw, come on, Jack. *Por favor.* I do it from Madrid's computer, and you say okay."

The passenger door slammed with abrupt, undue emphasis. Catherine Moore was standing outside the Tracker, her arms crossed in front of her, her expression a little reminiscent of a prosecuting attorney.

"Boys," Jack started, "we're going to have this conversation some other time, okay?"

The change of subject, he realized, was entirely unnecessary. They'd caught sight of Catherine's suede skirt, and, in typical thirteen-year-old reaction, they'd been struck dumb in the presence of someone so obviously of the opposite sex. Jack didn't wait for the next, equally predictable adolescent reaction. He scooted around the Tracker before they could start asking questions, took a firm hold of her elbow, and walked her into the front entryway of the apartment house, trying hard to ignore the palpable force of teenage imagination following them up the walkway.

"Friends of yours?" Catherine asked sweetly.

"Neighborhood kids," he told her. "Friends of your aunt's, I think."

"Yes, I should think so. Good friends, I guess. Using her computer with you."

At the end of the block, behind a delivery truck, the white convertible was parked.

Jack glanced at Catherine. Banked, seething anger was clear in every line of her set chin and clenched jaw. In her preoccupation with throttling him, Jack figured, she hadn't noticed the convertible, but that probably wouldn't make much difference to their persistent friend. The shady dealer would move in on her two seconds after Jack himself was out of the picture.

He stopped her at the door, turned her toward him, and smiled into her stormy brown eyes. "Tell you what, Professor," he said, groping for a deal she couldn't refuse. "You invite me in and give me a drink, and I'll explain all this."

She didn't want to trust him. He could see that. Her antipathy went beyond wariness to suspicion. She didn't lie worth a damn, but she knew she was about to be conned, and she didn't like it one bit.

But there was something else in her face. A hint of uncertainty and a touch of vulnerability. She was pursuing a Cause, and she wouldn't—couldn't—leave any stone unturned in her quest.

He was counting on it.

She hesitated long enough to make him worry about whether he'd played her right, then her bottom lip trembled just slightly before she bit down on it, raised her chin, and met his duplicitous gaze.

"All right," she said softly.

She turned away, fished in her shoulder bag for her keys, and unlocked the front door.

God, the woman was a sitting duck when it came to manipulation. There was no way he could allow her to fall into Blasquo's hands.

Or any hands besides his own.

The image that thought produced wafted through him with a concomitant rise in body heat. Neither was more mature than the adolescent reaction he'd just led her away from.

Jack frowned. His thoughts didn't take much analysis, he told himself. Just pure sex. Wasn't it? That uncertainty, that vulnerability didn't enter into it, did they?

He followed her in, watching her stiff, straight back and bravely squared, half-uncovered shoulders, telling himself in non-arguable terms that he'd had no choice but to fabricate a story. If *he* wasn't lying to her, Blasquo's crony would be. And everybody's neck would be in a sling. Including his.

So why did he feel so guilty about the whole damn situation?

Pure sex, Jack decided grimly, was getting a hell of a lot more complicated than he remembered.

Catherine didn't wait to see if he was following her.

In truth, she wasn't sure inviting him in had been such a good decision. She didn't trust him as far as she could throw a stone codex, and she'd probably be better off *not* hearing the explanation he'd offered. But he'd gone to considerable trouble to dissuade her from her search for information, had even lied to her in two languages, and she *had* to know why. Even if Madrid's troubles didn't come into it. It was a matter of female pride.

She walked past the small hallway lined with bookcases to the living room without bothering to describe the apartment's layout. Jack Gibraltar didn't need a tour guide. He'd been there before, and more than "once or twice." The kids hanging around outside Madrid's apartment were proof of that.

She turned to face him, crossing her arms in front of her and waiting for the explanation.

He ambled into the living room, leaned against the archway that led to the hall, and gave her a bland and innocent look, as if he had dropped in on a whim and was casting about for a conversational tidbit.

Catherine clamped her jaw and swallowed her frustration like a dose of cod liver oil. The chances of getting truthful answers from Jack Gibraltar were slim enough as it was. She wasn't going to invite him to lie to her by asking the questions. It was a small distinction, but it was a distinction nonetheless. And she didn't intend to give Jack Gibraltar an inch more than she had to.

After five seconds of silence he cleared his throat politely. "You going to offer me a drink?"

"Help yourself." She waved a hand in no particular direction.

He crossed unerringly to the liquor cabinet, filled two glasses with ice from the small refrigerator, and poured scotch into one of them. "You'll have ginger ale?" he asked her, looking up.

"Scotch," she told him, the single word slapped down like a gauntlet. Scotch was her aunt's drink of choice, not Catherine's, but the idea that Jack and Madrid shared something else in common from which Catherine was excluded stuck in her craw. She would have drunk radiator coolant if that was what he was drinking himself.

He gave her a pained smile, filled the second glass, and handed it to her.

Catherine took a sip and worked on acquiring a taste for it. Not ginger ale, but it was better than cod liver oil. By a long shot.

A little like unpalatable truth, she decided. Difficult to swallow, but preferable to bland, don't-worry-about-it banalities. She'd had enough of those after her mother had died to last a couple of lifetimes. All well meant and kind, but none of them capable of taking away pain or easing loneliness.

Or erasing her misgivings about Gibraltar.

She watched him take a hefty swallow of his drink and gather his wits, no doubt getting his story straight before he started talking.

He smiled at her, oozing sex appeal. That was the trouble with Jack Gibraltar, she decided warily. He was *too* attractive. With his rugged looks and rakish way, he was a man who could lure teenagers and bar patrons and senior archaeologists into eating out of his hands.

She braced herself against letting that blue-eyed charm tap her on the shoulder and invite itself into her confidence. It would be all too easy to succumb, she admitted. This man must have wiles that could get to her too.

If she wasn't careful.

She crossed her arms again, propping her glass in the crook of her arm. "The deal was that you were going to talk," she said.

"Mmm. The deal was that you were going to give me a drink too. On the other hand, getting it myself seemed like a good idea. I was afraid you'd lace it with arsenic."

"And deprive your computer-happy friends of their beloved mentor? Amazing how attached they've gotten to you after seeing you only *once or twice*."

"Mmm," he said again, though this one was morc of an irritated growl. "Those kids . . . they live in the neighborhood. Madrid befriended them. You know how she likes kids."

He waited for her to nod. It was going to be a long wait. She wondered if he thought she'd be happy with that kind of sketchy "explanation."

"She . . . ah . . . let them use the computer from time to time." He shrugged. "They got to know me because I was here working on the computer. They like the idea that I'm a hacker for a living, I guess. You know how kids are."

Catherine continued staring at him, then, grudgingly, nodded. She did know how kids were. They might like the idea of a computer hacker who'd made good, but they didn't bestow their hero worship lightly, and it was clear there was a case of hero worship going on between Jack and his teenage crew.

It was point in his favor, she conceded. A man who was hero to a bunch of adolescents had to have some stellar qualities. Though God knew what he was teaching them. And she doubted that their mothers would totally approve of his alterations to their computer files.

"Why were you here so often that the kids had a chance to get to know you?"

"We were deciphering a code. Running a few mathematical programs to try to figure out the numbers on the codex. It wasn't complex stuff computerwise. All the really tough jobs I did at home."

"On the computer you won't give me access to."

"Lady," he said with exaggerated patience, "I'd rather risk arsenic in my drink than have some amateur tiptoeing through my hard drive, all right?"

She felt the insult to her professionalism like a splash of cold water in her face. She *wasn't* an amateur. Archaeology libraries, dammit, had computers, and she'd been using them since she was an undergraduate! "Believe me, if I ever get access to your hard drive, I'm not planning to tiptoe!" she snapped.

"Well," he said, raising his drink to her in a mock toast, "you're honest. I'll give you that."

Irritation burned through her as she realized she'd just cooked her own goose when it came to his letting her see his computer files. "That's not what I—"

"Yes, it is. You have a tendency to say whatever you mean. Unedited." He took a sip of the scotch, watching her over the rim, checking out the look on her face, evaluating her in terms she had no doubt were his and his alone.

Catherine counted to ten, timing it by the pulse beats hammering away in her throat, then let out her breath in a long, careful sigh. "Maybe you ought to try the approach, Mr. Gibraltar. It usually works, unless you've got something to hide."

He rattled the ice in his glass, then rubbed the back of his neck with one hand. "Believe me, Cathy," he said, "I have your interest at heart here."

Cathy? Catherine frowned, taken off guard as much by the note of sincerity in the softly spoken words as by the nickname nobody had called her since she was seven years old.

"You don't want to get mixed up with Blasquo," he told her.

"Why not?"

"Because he plays in the big league. You cross him and he might just rearrange your living room with a minor explosive."

"My living room's insured."

"Yeah? What happens if you're in it when he does the rearranging?"

"Oh, come now, Mr. Gibraltar, that's really a little—"

"Come now yourself, *Professor*. Blasquo's a shark who eats archaeologists for breakfast, and you'd better believe that."

No, she told herself, watching his face, fighting her own troubling sense that he was, in this at least, telling her the truth. She wasn't going to start believing him. She couldn't afford to. "Is that what happened to my aunt? She got eaten by a shark?"

He went through the ice-rattling hand-on-the-back-of-his-neck routine again, then raked his hand through his hair—a gesture she was beginning to recognize as con-man's frustration. "No. No. Nothing like that. Madrid is nobody's idea of breakfast."

The frustration, she reflected with her hand fisted, was something they shared. A kindred emotion. "So what is she—one of the predators?"

"I didn't say that."

"You haven't *said* anything!" she flung out. "Nothing I can corroborate anyway, except that you're an honorary member of a teenage gang, and you're very protective of your hard drive!"

There was a moment of silence while she answered him stare for stare, and a muscle in his jaw tightened as if he were clenching his teeth hard enough to crack fillings.

When his eyes flicked down over her body, then met hers again, they glowed with the sensual knowledge that he'd taken in all the essentials. "You want to get your hands on my hard drive, *querida*?"

Ignore it, she told herself. There was no logical reason she should let herself react to the outrageous implication. But the thrill of excitement she felt in her pulse wasn't logical. Nothing about her reaction to this man had been logical from the moment she'd set eyes on him and he'd slammed a door in her face. "Are you sure you'd want to put it in the hands of an *amateur*?"

His voice was a little husky, as if it held too much scotch. "I don't know, Cathy, but it's an interesting thought."

On her name his voice lowered, that breath of emotion sending an unwarranted shiver down her spine. "The name," she said tightly, "is *Catherine*."

"Sorry."

He didn't sound repentant.

He didn't even sound polite. He sounded ironic and possibly a little smug, and when she shot him a sharp look she caught a slight, slow, masculine grin creeping up the corners of his mouth, crinkling the Elvis-blue eyes, and having the oddest effect on her breathing. Not to mention her intelligence and her better judgment.

She shut her eyes again, blocking out that too-seductive smile. "If you've finished your drink, Mr. Gibraltar, I think you'd better go."

The smile faded slowly, taking too much time. He glanced over his shoulder at the door, then looked back again. "Maybe we could—"

"No, I don't think we could," she said hastily, cutting him off, then regretting that she'd left the possibilities unsaid. Her imagination didn't need any more fuel than it already had.

"Cathy," he started again. His hand went to the back of his neck. "I don't think you really want to—"

"Mr. Gibraltar—" she said when he made no move toward the door.

He leaned back a little from the waist, as if he were evaluating her determination, then, apparently giving in, he shrugged and grinned at her again with that nearly irresistible charm.

"Okay. You want me to go, I'm out of here. I'll just go start the old rattletrap, and I'm gone."

"Fine."

He left his glass on a bookcase, shoved his hands into the pockets of his leather jacket, and let himself out the door, whistling softly.

Catherine's shoulders drooped in relief. He was gone, and she let herself feel a smidgen of satisfaction that she'd actually taken control of the situation—and the man.

The satisfaction didn't last any longer than it took for him to close the outside door, because it occurred to her then that Jack Gibraltar was not a man to be disposed of in two sentences—if being disposed of wasn't in his plan.

He'd given in too easily, when they both knew she'd been . . . susceptible. She had to admit it if she was honest. And she was.

Even if he wasn't.

She was frowning when she stepped to the front window and yanked back the curtain.

Jack Gibraltar had the hood up on the Tracker and was leaning over the fender, screwdriver in hand. He was removing something from the "rattletrap's" engine.

FOUR

His lips still pursed though he was no longer whistling, Jack slipped the distributor cap into the pocket of his leather jacket. He glanced once more toward the spot where the convertible had been parked. The car was gone, but Jack didn't have any illusions about the driver's loss of interest. He'd be back.

And he wasn't going to find Catherine Moore alone in her aunt's apartment just ripe for . . . whatever the sleazeball had in mind. He wasn't absolutely sure what that was, but he had some ideas.

Catherine Moore was a woman to give a man ideas all right.

Jack slammed the hood closed, shot one more steely glance toward the place where the convertible had been, then jogged up the walkway to her door and knocked.

She opened it as if she'd been waiting for him. He glanced up from his feet, taken off balance by her quickness.

She was waiting for him all right, but the emotion that burned just beneath her skin wasn't the passion of womanly welcome. She was seething. Anger emanated from her like the electric pulses of a bug lamp. If he'd been a mosquito, he would have been fried. And she wasn't going to invite him in on the basis of garden-variety charm. She looked ready to strangle him. Arsenic was clearly, in her mind, too tame a course of action.

She had, however, opened the door. If necessary, he could always put his foot in it.

He waited until she'd met his eyes with her own darkly flashing gaze, then stated with scrupulous if outrageous honesty, "My truck won't start."

"Oh?"

"That's right. Won't even turn over."

"Oh," she said again. Her breathing was a little quicker than normal, the small movement of her chest all too noticeable above the sliding neckline.

Jack leaned one arm against the doorjamb and bent toward her a little. "I thought you might let me come in and use your phone," he suggested.

"Who," she said pointedly, "are you going to call?"

"The garage."

She stepped back finally. "By all means," she told him, gesturing to the phone.

Casting her a wary glance, Jack crossed to the phone, made the call, then listened to it ring four times before he hung up. "No answer," he told her.

"Somehow, that doesn't surprise me."

No doubt about it. Catherine Moore had his number.

The observation wasn't earthshaking. She'd probably been watching him out the window.

It didn't take much to picture her standing with one suede-draped hip against the window frame, leaning out over the sill in that loose blouse. He shut his eyes for a moment, mentally shaking his head at himself. He should have checked before he raised the hood. He should have known.

Hell, maybe he had known. Maybe he'd wanted to get her angry enough to feel the heat, the kind of fire that delivered on the promises she didn't know she was making every time her temper flared and a wash of color tinted her skin.

He pushed his hands into his pockets and locked her stormy gaze on to his. "You have something you want to say?" he asked softly.

She resisted for five seconds, then her seething anger won out over her composure. "Yes," she gritted at him. "A little mechanical advice, since the garage doesn't answer. If you put that little doodad back under your hood, you might have more success with starting it."

He let out a breath and pulled the distributor cap out of his pocket. "This one?"

"Yes."

"It's a distributor cap."

"How enlightening."

"You don't want enlightenment."

Her furious gaze dropped to his throat. She was thinking about strangling *and* dismemberment, he guessed. And the flush that rushed just under her skin was damn near irresistible.

"You want an apology?"

"No! I want an explanation."

The corner of his mouth turned up an inch. "Well, that one's easy, *querida*," he said. "I wanted to spend the night."

"You wanted to—" The rest of her sentence vanished into a catch in her breath. Another blaze of heat highlighted her face. "You wanted to spend the night?" she said, her voice disbelieving. "So you just . . . concocted a story and pulled some doodad out of your truck? And I'm supposed to—"

The small pulse at the base of her throat had quickened. Jack watched it, fascinated, aware that he was within reaching distance of her. "I don't know what you're supposed to do. What do you want to do?"

She was clutching her drink as if it were the only thing holding her up. "*Not* spend time with you!"

"Then why did you let me in?"

"I thought I might force you to speak some truth! I should have known better. You wouldn't know the truth if it booted up your computers and reconfigured your system!" She took a breath that disturbed the neckline of her blouse, though it steadied her voice. "If then."

"No?" He caught her gaze. "You want to talk about hard drives again?"

Her eyes widened, and her throat worked in a small, revealing movement he would have missed if he hadn't been watching for it so intensely. But he was, and he couldn't miss the signs. She hadn't brought up his computer by accident, even if she thought she had. What she was feeling was the excitement she couldn't quite shut off, even if it scared her.

It was the same flash of excitement he'd seen in her eyes in La Stela, when she'd stared back at him and met his challenge with one of her own. She knew she was playing with the kind of fire her life hadn't prepared her to handle. But she couldn't resist it. She was drawn to it by something in her nature that was just waking up. She was a crusader, and the passion that fueled a quest was coursing through her now, taking her in a very different direction.

It was a direction that fired Jack's blood as much as it did hers. Enough to make him forget that her quest for the truth could nail him to the wall, and that playing with Catherine was something he couldn't afford to get burned on.

"Here's the truth, *querida*," he said, his voice a low, masculine rumble. "You knew what I wanted when you gave me that look of yours, back in the bar, talking about who was buying."

"That's . . . ridiculous." The second word trailed off in a gasp that Jack felt all the way down to his jeans.

"Is it?" He gave her a chance to answer the challenge, then murmured into the humming silence, "Here's some more of that truth you claim you're looking for. You knew what you wanted too."

"I think," she said as if her voice might break glass, "you should leave."

"Maybe I should, but that's not the question." He took a step closer to her.

"That's exactly—"

"The question is whether you want me to."

He let it hang in the air while he watched her chin rise and her shoulders drop in acceptance of what he was saying. She let the moment for denying it go by, unused.

"I don't think you do. And I think you're woman enough to admit it."

"I—" He saw the brief struggle for convenient deception, then the deeper, more intense hold of honest emotion.

He reached out and gently took her glass from her fingers before she spilled the contents onto her aunt's favorite Mayan rug.

"You going to tell me you don't want me to touch you, Cathy?"

She watched him set the glass down on the bookcase, then her gaze followed his hand as he brought it up to her shoulder and slowly brushed her hair back from her neck.

It was the lightest of touches, but she shivered and caught her breath in a sound that was half gasp, half whisper.

Jack felt such a surge of need flow through him that he gritted his teeth against it, shocked himself at the force.

God, she had the kind of skin that wanted to be caressed, that would give back sensual impressions like slow, tingling electric current. And she was the kind of woman who would look into a man's eyes and let him see what it would feel like when he slid his fingers just inside the back of that suede skirt.

In slow motion he trailed his fingers across the curve of her shoulder, barely touching her, just taking in the texture and heat of her skin. As if it were inevitable, he took the last step toward her, pulled his hand out of his pocket, slid it behind her hair at the back of her neck, exerting faint pressure to tip her head up to his. Her eyes were wide, her mouth vulnerable with indecision. He knew, though, what she'd taste like when he kissed her.

And he knew he wasn't going to be able to stop himself. With a final silent pointless excuse to that part of himself that knew he was treading on dangerous ground, he lowered his head down over hers and covered her mouth with his.

Catherine didn't resist him. There was no real possibility that she would. She didn't want to. She wanted him to touch her, to kiss her, to fit their mouths together so closely she could feel his breath mingle with hers.

She knew that tipping her head back against his hand when he burrowed his fingers deeper into her hair was foolish, but she couldn't for the life of her make herself push him away. She was letting him seduce her, but there was a heady sense of female power that contradicted all the protests she knew she should utter.

His arm tightened around her back, and when she parted her lips for the warm, eager glide of his tongue, the rumble he made in the back of his throat turned her bones to water.

It was crazy. It was foolhardy. It was . . . illogical, but she couldn't summon any shred of common sense beyond a faint "Jack . . ." sighed against his mouth.

"Yes, Cathy. Ah, yes, that's right, let me know what you mean."

Let him know what she meant? She didn't

know herself. She didn't know anything beyond the sweet tangle of sensations his kiss evoked.

He ran his palms roughly up the back of her blouse to her bare shoulders, pulling her toward him. Against the top of her breasts the cool, slick leather of his jacket and the coarse cotton of his shirt were incredibly erotic, burning a trail through her. She wrapped her arms around his back and pressed her fingers into the hollow of his spine.

There was no way to explain her sudden uncharacteristic reaction. She just knew she wanted what was happening to her. She *demanded* it. She was taking it.

"Oh, yes, babe, do that again," he murmured.

She realized she'd slid his shirt out of his jeans. She hadn't meant to do that, she told herself even as she slipped her hands inside the back of his shirt, seeking warm, bare, heated skin.

"And this." His hands cupped her backside, pulled her against the junction of his thighs, and demonstrated what she'd been doing with her hips. Even through layers of denim and suede she could feel what the intimate contact had done to him.

He rocked against her, and his breath came

out in a low moan. "God, that is sweet. Ah . . . Cathy. *Estás dulce. Sí, otra vez . . .*"

He continued murmuring in Spanish, and the words took her by surprise—but not nearly as much as the wave of exquisite pleasure that fanned out from their bodies. Caught between the cool leather of his jacket and the hot intensity of his hands, she let her back arch, and her head tipped back against his guiding palm. The faint taste of scotch on his mouth was unexpectedly sweet, the Spanish the most intimately exotic words she'd ever heard.

No one had ever made love to her in Spanish.

Not even men who knew she spoke the language.

She had the craziest urge to whisper his Spanish love words back to him, to tell him that for her, too, it had never been like this, that she couldn't resist him. The craziest conviction that what she said would be true in any language, that the rogue computer hacker who'd been lying to her all night was telling her something she couldn't doubt, in a universal language.

She'd wanted truth. She wanted it now. And there was no denying that what was happening between them was Truth with a capital T.

"*Sí, otra vez,*" she murmured. "*Quiero cantar una canción de mi corazón . . . contigo . . .*"

"*Te entiendo. Quisiera cantar contigo . . .*" He kissed her again, his hands roving up to her shoulders to cup the back of her head in a passionate grip. Then slowly he unwrapped his fingers and lifted his head to gaze down at her. A frown began to crease his forehead.

Catherine stared up at him, wanting his mouth back on hers, realizing he was looking at her strangely, coming to some unexpected conclusions.

"*Hablas español, querida?*" he muttered, frowning harder.

"*Sí. Hablo español.*"

"You do?" The significance of her answer scrolled across his face. He looked a little stunned.

A small surge of satisfaction rippled through her at the fact that she'd outdueled him, in a small way, on his Spanish fast-talk. But the thrill of satisfaction was overwhelmed by the inexplicable urge to meet him on a more sensual field of combat than wits. She couldn't stop herself from leaning a little toward him, angling her neck to the side to brush against his fingers.

He peered at her as if she were some species he didn't know quite what to do with, but his hands gripped her upper arms as if he'd never let her go. "You mean . . . outside the bar. Your friend who followed us . . ."

She nodded.

"*Socorreme Dios*. You are something, *querida*."

His voice was rough with desire, his eyes darkened to a deep, stormy sea blue she could have fallen into. She'd never met a man who appealed so much to her senses or her imagination, or to some rogue, lawless part of herself that wanted to whisper Spanish love words in his ear all night long while he made reckless, passionate love to her on Madrid's Mayan rug.

The idea sent illicit shivers down her spine. She was a sigh away from giving in to them, and she knew it.

"What . . . are you doing?" she said a little breathlessly as his hands began moving up.

"I'm getting you closer, so you won't be able to tell me anything I don't want to hear right now."

She flattened her hands against his chest. "But maybe we should . . . talk . . ."

"Unh-unh. I don't want to talk." He slid his hands into her hair and tipped her head to the side to give his mouth access to the tingling, sensitive erogenous nerves at the side of her neck. "Not in English anyway."

She didn't want to talk either. She wanted to feel that deep, exquisite ache in the very center of her being. To thrill to the intoxicating knowledge that she was doing the same thing to him. That they were both swept up in this breathless, exotic passion neither one of them could . . .

Could what? Control? That wasn't true, she told herself breathlessly. Catherine Moore did not lose control, even in the heat of . . . whatever it was she was in the heat of. Something describable only in another language, no doubt. She'd lost her head when she started speaking Spanish.

And what then? After a night of Spanish love, would he put the doodad back in his truck and drive off? Leaving her uninformed and thwarted in her purpose and as frustrated as before?

Jack stopped for a moment, pulled back, then closed his eyes and shook his head. "No. Don't turn crusader on me now, Cathy."

"Crusader?"

"Cathy," he murmured in a husky voice, "I know you have a mission. But trust me, it can wait for tomorrow."

Trust him? Trust a man with a distributor cap in his jacket pocket?

And the worst part was that she wanted to. She almost did. She wanted nothing more than to melt into Jack Gibraltar's arms and let him convince her that the night was all that mattered. She'd never responded to a man this way before.

It was an act of God that the phone started to ring. She wasn't at all sure what she would have done if it hadn't. As it was, she made only the smallest movement toward freeing herself.

Jack groaned in her ear, the stirring of his breath a seductive plea that reached directly to that part of her clamoring for more of his attentions, but she held herself stiff and suppressed her shiver of response.

Reluctantly, he let go of her. She almost stumbled, pushing herself away from him, then quickly crossed the room to the phone as if she were afraid he'd change his mind.

Her breathless "Hello?" sounded as if she'd sprinted halfway across Chetumal.

A polite masculine voice responded. "Buenas noches. Is this Catherine Moore?"

"Yes."

"This is Esteban Blasquo."

Blasquo? She made an effort to organize her confused thoughts, trying to assimilate the fact that Blasquo was calling her at her aunt's number. It didn't quite make sense. "Oh. Yes, I've . . . wanted to speak to you, Mr. Blasquo. About the codex."

There was a regretful pause. "Excuse me, señorita. But I do not wish to speak to *you* about this subject."

"You . . . don't?" *Then why was he calling?*

"Actually," Blasquo continued, "I would like to speak to Mr. Gibraltar."

Jack Gibraltar? She glanced up at him, frowning, feeling reality jolt into place and banish the debilitating sensuality she'd almost succumbed to moments before. She let out a long breath, raising her chin. "I wasn't aware he'd left this number with anyone," she said.

There was a polite laugh. "I usually know how to reach him."

"Oh?"

"We are good friends."

"Good friends?"

Jack Gibraltar was frowning back at her, his eyes warily shifting from the phone to her face.

"Is he available, señorita?"

Catherine held the receiver out, hooking her free thumb into her skirt. "It's for you."

"For me?"

"Mr. Blasquo." She forced a smile. "Surely you remember him. The man you described as a shark who eats archaeologists for breakfast?"

"Yes, well . . ."

"He *claims* you're good friends."

Jack expressed a polite interest in Mr. Blasquo's health, responded to a similar inquiry, said yes twice, confirmed a date and time, and hung up.

Then he turned around to face the woman who three minutes earlier had been melting in his arms.

One glance told him she'd stopped melting. She was holding herself very straight, her arms crossed in front of her, her hands wrapped around her elbows in a defensive gesture. Pride had squared her shoulders and lifted her chin, but her wide, passionate brown eyes glinted with the kind of emotion that would have done credit to Joan of Arc.

Jack sighed. Nothing like passionate, burn-at-the-stake idealism to change the mood.

"What did Mr. Blasquo want?" she asked him.

Jack took a deep breath, sifted through the range of possible answers, and gave her the truth. "He wanted to discuss the codex."

"But not," she said evenly, "with me."

He let out his breath, then grinned, flicking his gaze lower for a moment. "No accounting for taste."

Her throat worked in an involuntary response, but she wasn't having any of it. "Stop that."

"Stop what?"

"Trying to distract me. It won't work. At least not . . . now."

Not now? Now that she was six feet away from him instead of pressed against him and moaning in his ear? He shoved his hands into his pockets, rocked back on his heels, and contemplated her. "That's what I am? A . . . distraction?"

"We won't go into what you are," she told him.

"A few minutes ago I was your soulmate in a song of the heart, if I translated it correctly, *querida*."

"That was just . . ."

"Just *what*?" He watched as a flush spread all the way down to the low neckline.

"All right!" she said, surprising him. "We both know what it was." Her eyes met his, the honesty in them hitting him straight in the gut. "And it's not something we're going to repeat!"

He wanted, badly, to close the gap between them, pull her sweet body against his, and do just that—repeat what they both knew it was. Prove her wrong.

Instead, he moved toward the bookcase, picked up Catherine's discarded drink, and took a long pull at the scotch. "Listen, *querida*—"

"And you can stop talking to me in Spanish!"

"Why?"

"Because . . . because . . ."

Because she liked it? Jack's response to that thought tightened every muscle in his body.

"Because that's the language you used to utterly misrepresent my purposes to that man I was talking to outside the bar! Not to mention utterly mistranslating his approaches to me!"

"Right," Jack muttered, irritated by the glib statement of fact. He didn't expect that from Catherine. Glossing over the truth was *his* game, dammit, not hers.

And when he was with her he wasn't even sure he wanted to play it. He had the urge to dispense with his careful constructions of the facts and just tell her what the hell was going on. He looked at her for a moment, considering it.

Coming clean. Watching those wide brown eyes lose that judgmental, self-righteous censure and seeing it replaced with the emotion that burned just beneath her smooth, warm, ivory skin.

"The man outside the bar," he said slowly, trying it out. "He was Blasquo's agent. He wasn't after an honest business deal."

"Oh? Mr. Blasquo the shark? Your good friend?"

"Mr. Blasquo isn't a friend," he said. "He doesn't even *think* he's a friend."

"Then what does he want?"

He took another drink of scotch. "He wants to pick my brain, I imagine."

She took that in. "Well," she said, "maybe he'll have better luck than I had."

She held herself perfectly still, her back

straight, her chin raised, her gaze linked with his. She had the kind of eyes—deep and soft—a man could fall into, Jack thought.

He stopped himself just in time, pulling himself back from the brink with another mouthful of scotch and a mental kick in the pants.

What the hell was he doing?

If he got carried away with this sudden need for honesty, he'd end up with a treasured part of his anatomy in a sling. In which case his chances of sharing it with Catherine Moore would be nil.

When he'd made his public announcement about the codex, he'd known he was only buying time. And what Jack needed to do now was buy a little more time.

Which was going to be exceedingly difficult with Catherine watching him from across the room, wheels turning in her head, crusader's passion ruling her heart.

And her blouse slipping off her shoulders again.

Distraction wasn't the word, he thought warily. *Ambushed*, *knocked down*, and *taken by storm* were the words. Whispered in his ear. In Spanish.

Damn. He couldn't remember the last time

he'd met a woman who affected him this way with a total lack of intent.

"Listen, Cathy," he started. "I don't think you have to worry about your aunt. I mean, she's off . . . somewhere . . ."

Her mouth firmed into a line that looked determined not to finish his sentences, then her lips twitched at one corner and she muttered, "The Mexican Riviera. Cancún, or someplace."

"Yeah. Right." He rubbed the back of his neck. "Madrid's lying in the sun, on an extended sabbatical, and when she's ready to work again, she'll come back with a tan. Nobody's been fired. Nobody's even been asked to leave. And it's my best guess she's a lot less worried about this whole scene than you are."

"I'm not worried about it," she said, but before he could utter a sigh of relief she added, "I just want to know what's really going on."

He covered his eyes with one hand. "Archaeologists get fooled. It happens all the time."

"I'm sure it happens to some of them all the time. But my aunt?"

She had a point, Jack admitted silently. Madrid was shrewd. She wouldn't have been fooled by any kind of ordinary mistake.

"Believe me," he muttered, "no one could have caught on to this particular forgery."

"You apparently did."

"Yeah. Well, that was . . . later." He shot her a glance. "Hindsight. You know?"

She didn't even blink. No, she didn't know, Jack figured. But she was going to find out. If it killed her.

She'd probably turn up on Blasquo's doorstep the minute Jack turned his back on her. Jack rattled the ice in the glass, drained the scotch, and set the empty glass down on the bookcase, slanting Catherine a look.

There was no way this crusading idealist was going to go back to her library and stay out of trouble as long as she had options left.

He shut his eyes for a moment, swearing silently. He just couldn't afford to let that happen.

"Look," he said, glancing at her. "You want to talk to Blasquo?"

"Of course."

"All right, then. You come with me tomorrow night. As my date."

"Your . . . date?"

She sounded so incredulous, he had to go back over the plan in his mind before he repeated it. He told himself he knew what he was doing.

Keeping her out of trouble. Setting up a deal where he could watch two birds with one stone. Anticipating the advice he knew he'd get from the other end of this plan. Protecting a highly valued and underinsured con game.

It had nothing to do with wanting to get his hands on her again.

"That's the only way you'll get into Blasquo's dinner party," he said brusquely.

"A ruse, you mean."

"Yeah."

She caught her lip between her teeth, worrying it in a way Jack found unnerving. That and the fact that Catherine carrying out any kind of ruse was questionable at best. She was the worst liar in creation.

"You think you can manage that?" he asked her.

She bristled. "Of course I—" Her gaze slid away from him. "Well. I'll do whatever I have to do."

Meaning what? he wondered, irritated. That she could lower her standards enough to manage a little white lie? Or that going out on a date with him was personal sacrifice akin to being burned at the stake?

"Lady, the only thing I've seen you do so far is exactly what you want to do."

"That's hardly fair! You're the one who dragged me off in your truck and brought me here."

"It's where you were going anyway."

"Not without making some arrangement with a conveniently connected man whom you snatched away from me!"

He rolled his eyes. "You wanted to talk to Blasquo. All right. I'm giving you the chance to talk to him. As my date. All I ask is that you make it convincing."

"Just what did you have in mind?"

What did he have in mind?

She had to be kidding.

He flicked his gaze down over her, then raised one eyebrow. "You really want an answer to that one too, *querida*?"

"No!" she said hurriedly. "Let me make myself clear, Mr. Gibraltar. I have no intention of forming a relationship with you."

"Yeah, we discussed relationships before." Ten minutes ago, when she'd been calling him *mi amor* and pulling his shirt out of his pants.

"That kind of relationship would be untenable."

Untenable. God, he hated academics.

He hated them especially when they were right. He'd already told himself a relationship with Catherine Moore would be disastrous. She was persistent, dangerous, downright intrusive on his carefully laid plans. Furthermore, she did things to his logic circuits that didn't bode well for long-term self-preservation. What she was saying was absolutely right.

And it grated against every masculine impulse in his body.

Jack gritted his teeth and took another deep breath. "I'll pick you up here tomorrow, at three. All right?"

"Fine."

"Fine," he repeated.

She raised her chin at him.

He took another breath. "You're not going to . . . ah . . . go wandering around in the neighborhood in that outfit, are you?"

The neckline slipped a little, but she didn't make a move to fix it. "Why? Don't tell me you're still worried about the man in the convertible?"

"No. I'm pretty sure he reported back to Blasquo before we got our friendly phone call. But Ace and his buddies—they're at that impressionable age."

A wash of color tinted her cheeks. "They won't be *impressed* by me, Mr. Gibraltar."

"Good." Jack stuffed his hands into his pockets. "You're not going to wear it to Blasquo's dinner party either, I hope?"

She crossed her arms in front of her.

"He's impressionable too," Jack said.

"Anyone else you're worried I'll . . . impress?"

"Yeah," Jack muttered, heading toward the door. "Me."

FIVE

Catherine popped the tab on yet another can of soda, ripped open the last bag of potato chips, and handed them both to the teenager sitting in front of her aunt's computer. She hoped the one-pound bag of chips would keep Ace quiet. She was feeling guilty enough as it was. She didn't need a cheerful and apparently experienced commentary on the process of breaking into Madrid's computer from a young electronics vagrant who didn't appear to know the meaning of guilt.

She'd discovered him hanging around outside Madrid's apartment, keeping an eye out for a white convertible on Jack's orders. Her initial outrage had breezed by Ace like a Frisbee in a city park. Surveillance, in Ace's book, wasn't even a social faux pas, especially since it had been suggested by Jack Gibraltar.

"Jack would not have set it up without a password," Ace mumbled through a mouthful of chips.

Jack's methods were sacrosanct in Ace's book, and spoken of with awe for his ability to crack computer codes. Ace's hero had taught Ace all he knew, the teenager had informed her with reverence. When he'd offered to demonstrate his prowess, she'd looked hero worship in the face and known she didn't stand a chance of defeating it.

"He would use some word Madrid would remember, yes?" Ace said. The password Ace was searching for would get him into Madrid's message network which, Ace was sure, was interconnected with Jack's computers.

"Maybe she wrote it down."

"No. Jack would tell her not to."

"Far be it from anyone to countermand an edict from Jack."

Ace's glance indicated he couldn't translate the phrase, but he didn't ask for an explanation. Clearly he thought she was agreeing with him. The idea of anyone contradicting Jack wasn't thinkable. "If this were Jack here, he would know to get into the message board in five strokes." Ace went after another handful of chips. "He has—you know—fastest moves in the business."

"No kidding," Catherine commented.

He stopped munching, glanced at her, then looked away while his ears turned an intense shade of red. It was obvious he'd understood the innuendo with no trouble. "I mean . . . you know, computers. I did not mean . . ."

"No, of course not."

Though he had, of course. She'd put on baggy jeans and a sweatshirt before she'd invited him in, but Ace's impressionable thoughts didn't seem noticeably subdued by a change of wardrobe.

Neither did hers, for that matter. Ace was probably picking up stray emanations from the singed air in the living room.

"He would show you all this if he stayed. I mean," Ace added, "if he had spare hands, you know?" He squeezed his eyes shut and retreated into mortified mumbling. "Spare *time*. I mean spare time."

"More soda?" she asked diplomatically.

"*Sí. Por favor.*"

She headed for the kitchen in search of appropriate diversion for a bilingual teenager caught between dual obsessions with sex and computers. She got Ace another soda, then, on second thought, got one for herself too.

"Maybe it was an archaeological term," she suggested when she handed Ace the can.

Ace scowled at the screen.

"A word from her studies," Catherine said. "Try 'Maya,' or 'codex.' "

"Maya." Recognition came into the teenager's face. "*Sí*," he said. "The Maya. They invent zero, you know? Zero is half a computer."

Catherine's mouth quirked. It was an interesting view of history. She wondered if he'd gotten it from Jack.

"Okay," Ace mused, staring at the screen. "What would Jack do now?"

Something criminal, no doubt. "Ace," she said, "don't do anything that's going to get you in trouble."

"No. Jack would not turn us in anyway."

"I wouldn't be too—"

"He did not turn us in when he caught us—you know—breaking his truck."

That stopped her for a moment. "You broke into his truck?"

"*Sí*," Ace said with no compunction. "We want his disks—from the computer. We want to see what is on them."

Maybe you don't want to know this, Catherine, she thought uneasily. "What *was* on them?"

Ace shrugged. "We get caught. He gave us a looong lecture about the future. He tells us we must be respectable. Not like him, you know, when he is a kid. In trouble."

She wasn't interested, Catherine told herself. She didn't want to hear Jack's history. She was susceptible enough to Jack Gibraltar as it was. An ounce of sympathy and a blue-eyed grin, and the next thing she knew she'd be whispering Spanish nothings to a man with a distributor cap in his pocket.

"What kind of trouble?" she asked.

The teenager dug into the chips again. "His family, they divorce, you know? And they fight over him."

"In a custody battle?"

"*Sí.* In the court. So Jack runs away to steal cars. Then this . . . worker . . . *asistente social* . . ."

"A social worker?"

"*Sí.* Social worker. She teaches him computers, and now he goes straight."

"He does?" Catherine put in warily. Probing her aunt's computer files put her on shaky enough ground. Probing into Jack's previous life was even shakier. Especially as told through the eyes of a kid who clearly worshipped him.

"This is why he teaches us computers," Ace said. "He makes us promise not to break any more trucks. So we go straight. Like him."

Catherine took a long breath and clamped

her mouth shut on the questions she was dying to ask. She didn't want to know this, she told herself. She couldn't *afford* to know anything more about a man whose message board she was trying to break into at this very moment.

"I think you're losing your file, Ace," Catherine said hurriedly.

Ace glanced back to the computer and sighed as information scrolled off the screen. "Maya is not the word," he reported.

"Oh. Well, then—"

"What is the other word?"

She hesitated. "Codex."

Ace repeated the word and she nodded absently. She hadn't known Jack's checkered history. Or that he'd been a kid in trouble. Or that now he helped other kids headed down the same road.

The teenager frowned. "He did not tell you about when he runs away from home?" he asked.

She shook her head.

"Well," he said offhandedly, "maybe he does not want you to know. Maybe he wants you to think he is always straight. Maybe he thinks if you know his trouble, you will not want to—" He stopped, obviously realizing that the direction of his thoughts was all too clear. "I mean . . ."

"That's okay, Ace," Catherine assured him. "And about the computer . . ."

"*Hola,*" Ace said, sitting up a little straighter.

Catherine stared at the computer screen and saw what he had typed in. "Code X?"

"*Sí.*" He grinned at her, social embarrassment lost in technological triumph. "*Perfectamente.* Look."

Staring at his computer screen, Jack hit a few keys and called up a program. An archaeological satellite scan, computer enhanced in garish colors, glowed on the screen. He typed in a few more commands, made some minor but crucial adjustments to the map, and sent it to his printer. He checked it as it came out of the machine, nodding once. It was a perfectly usable piece of misinformation. If Blasquo had any ideas of raiding the apartment while he was entertaining Jack for dinner, there might as well be something for him to find.

The falsified satellite scan should take care of providing a distraction at this end. On the dinner party side, Catherine should provide enough distraction for everyone concerned. All Jack had to do was figure out a way to keep the crusader-on-a-mission from learning anything—and she seemed awfully good at learning things.

Retiring for the moment that particular problem in the back of his mind, Jack picked up the doctored map and glanced around the apartment, wondering where to leave it that wouldn't be too obvious for Blasquo's friends. Then with a snort of derision, he carried it over to the iguana cage. He measured the printout against the rim, then folded the edges under to make it fit as a liner.

Archie, who hadn't yet forgiven Jack for removing him from a major street and paying the local vet holiday weekend rates to set his broken leg, made a predictable and nerve-racking attempt to defend his territory.

Jack pulled his hand out in the nick of time. Archie eyed him with malevolence and stumped toward the back of the cage, dragging his cast awkwardly.

"Hey," Jack pointed out. "I wasn't the one trying to cross Route Two."

Archie didn't make any attempt to defend his intelligence.

There probably wasn't any defense, Jack decided. Pesos to pancakes, there was a female in the picture. In which case Archie's intelligence, such as it was, didn't stand a chance.

Jack met the baleful neon-green stare with a grimace of his own. "I just hope for your sake your lady friend's not a crusader, buddy. Though she probably is. You've got all the symptoms."

Archie blinked.

Jack shut his eyes, wondering about his own symptoms as he sat back down in front of the computer and called up another file.

For a man who was trying to run a dicey scam, he was spending an inordinate amount of time thinking about Catherine Moore. But, God, she'd acted as if she'd never before been carried away by a man's hands on her bare shoulders, a man's mouth on hers. As if all that passion had been held back, untapped, until he touched her. Just the thought of the soft, breathless sounds she'd made in the back of her throat—

He shook his head to clear it of the arousing memory and forcefully brought his attention back to the computer. He pressed a few keys, checked the screen, then called up his message board.

He blinked, frowned in disbelief, shook his head, and stared at the screen again.

A string of curses spewed out from Jack's lips. It didn't take much to figure what was going on.

Catherine. Ace. An available computer tied into his network.

That was the thing about a Woman With a Cause, Jack decided sourly, staring at his screen. She could be such a damn pain in the butt.

After staring at the closet for ten minutes, Catherine concluded she didn't have anything to wear to a dinner party hosted by a shark who may or may not be in collusion with her date.

Especially when she herself had joined the ranks of the ethically questionable.

A pang of guilt nagged its way into the back of her mind, brought on by the sight of Madrid's computer, now turned off and covered, in the corner of the room. No amount of justification had completely smoothed over her ruffled conscience. She'd always been a scrupulously honest person. She'd never in her life considered criminal invasion of privacy.

Or donning Aunt Madrid's native costumes and hawking antiquities on the street.

Or making love in Spanish.

Agitated, she turned away from the closet, walked out to the living room, and picked up

Ace's discarded soda cans. She tossed them into the trash in the kitchen while smothering another stray guilt gremlin. Shouldn't she be recycling it? What *did* Madrid do with all these cans?

She must discard enough aluminum to start her own recycling center, Catherine thought. Even Ace's computer-cracking thirst hadn't appreciably diminished the supply of soda in her aunt's refrigerator. She stocked it, of course, for Ace and his buddies.

Catherine pulled open the refrigerator door and got herself a ginger ale, then stared for a moment at the stacks of soda.

Madrid's refrigerator had been one of the fixtures of her childhood. Her aunt had always kept soda and potato chips on hand for those times when Catherine had needed to escape from the staid, all-male, strictly academic efficiency of her father's household.

Sometimes, when Catherine arrived unannounced, her aunt would be there. More often, now that she thought about it, there'd be a note tacked to the refrigerator, brief and to the point. The one she remembered most had said: *Dig. Peru.*

That was probably why Madrid got along so well with Jack Gibraltar, she decided.

Nobody had to answer awkward questions like where and when and did you leave a phone number?

She let go of the door. It swung shut with a soft wheeze.

What *were* they involved in?

The message on the network board had been even more cryptic than Madrid's refrigerator notes. *South 5.* It wouldn't have made any sense at all if Ace hadn't managed to call up that satellite scan—probably the last map Jack had worked on for her aunt. But with no coordinates, and no specific locations, it didn't tell her much.

She popped the top on her ginger ale so forcefully that liquid spurted out of the can and she had to hold it over the sink to keep it from spilling on the floor.

She'd *hated* those cryptic notes on the refrigerator, Catherine thought with uncharacteristic anger. She'd wanted to *know*, dammit!

The can stopped foaming, and Catherine turned around and leaned back against the sink. Her aunt's raided computer stared back at her, making accusations.

Sighing, she walked back to the closet. It probably didn't matter what she wore. As the uninvited guest of a man who had already refused to speak to her, she was unlikely to get any information anyway.

She reached for a garment she'd brought with her—a conservative linen-polyester suit that packed well and resisted stains. It was what she'd worn when she'd shown up on Jack Gibraltar's doorstep to politely appeal to his conscience.

Unfortunately, his conscience wasn't the part of his anatomy that had had the most practice.

Catherine took another sip of ginger ale, then held the cold can against her forehead. That first encounter with Jack was the start of her racy underground career, such as it was. That slammed door, those sexy blue eyes flicking down over her polyester-blend suit, his telling her that she belonged back at the library.

She'd had to prove him wrong. She might not be the glamorous, adventurous anarchist of the family, but she was more than just a staid, respectable college professor.

Jack Gibraltar's slammed door had sprung open one of her own. He'd stormed her guarded psyche and released impulses she'd never thought she had. And every infuriating remark and outrageous insinuation had freed a little more of her errant alter ego, flushed out a few more reckless urges until she'd found herself leaning into his leather-jacketed chest and whispering words of intoxicating possibilities into his ear.

He'd lit the fuse to a part of her she didn't quite recognize, and she wasn't sure where it would lead. Scandal? Academic censure?

The same place as Madrid, some stern warning voice in her head intoned. And where, pray tell, was that? What kind of trouble was she in?

South 5. Dammit, that was so *like* Madrid!

Catherine laid the suit on the bed and as she started toward the bathroom, she was suddenly arrested by a glimmer of an idea. It *was* like Madrid. The cryptic note, the unidentified dig site. It was a lot more like Madrid than lying under the sun, escaping her colleagues' censure. Her aunt wasn't on the Mexican Riviera. Ten to one Madrid was on a dig, pursuing some interest she hadn't bothered to share with the academic community at large, while her accomplice kept the computer scans coming and foiled Catherine with romance and rhetoric and dangerous possibilities.

She gazed at the computer, and unconsciously hooked her thumbs into the waistband of her jeans. She could call up the university computer and compare maps. Of course, there was no way to know for sure she'd have the right site.

Except by going there.

She snatched up the suit and thrust it back into the closet, then pulled out sweaters, shorts, chinos, Madrid's suede jacket, and the overnight bag she'd brought with her.

There were risks in the Yucatán. But they didn't compare to the risks she'd be taking if she saw Jack Gibraltar again, listened to him again, went on a date with him, for sweet heaven's sake!

She felt one final pang of conscience at the thought of standing up a man whose computer she'd just broken into, but she buried it under a stack of underwear and a couple of pairs of socks.

She'd leave him a note.

Dig—Campeche.

Jack yanked the note out from under its refrigerator magnet and scowled at it. What the hell did that mean? She'd gone on a dig in Yucatán?

Hell. He knew what it meant. She'd gotten the message in his network board, all right, and decided to pursue the piece of information right into the jaws of a whole school of sharks.

He gritted his teeth and massaged his temples, trying to rub away the conclusions that were, unfortunately, all too obvious.

She'd faked him out again. Dammit, for a crusader, she was developing a talent for larceny that was nothing short of awesome.

When he'd let her and Ace call up the doctored map, he hadn't intended her to *go* there. He'd just meant to give her some piece of information she could let slip to Blasquo while she was trying to lie about it, so that *he'd* go there.

Which he very well might.

And when he did, he'd run straight into Catherine.

Jack hissed a Spanish curse through his teeth. She'd gone way past trampling over a good con. If somebody didn't drag her away from her quest, she was going to turn herself into shark food.

There wasn't much argument about what he'd have to do next.

Dive in after her.

SIX

Heart slamming against her ribs, Catherine stared through the windshield of the rented Jeep. Her hands were clutched around the steering wheel, and her chin rested on the edge of the wheel, where she'd just banged it after stopping suddenly. Slowly her breathing returned to normal.

The view through the windshield consisted of a deep ditch cutting directly across the miserable path she'd been following for the past two hours. While she watched, the delicate miniature brocket deer she'd swerved to avoid leapt in front of the Jeep, paused a moment to blink in the headlights, then jumped gracefully across the trench and disappeared into the dense rain forest. The path Catherine was on also disappeared into that jungle.

She'd found the dig, she acknowledged grimly. Up close and personal.

The Jeep was canted at a forty-five-degree angle, one of its wheels buried in mud, one headlight glaring at a trickle of running water, the other aimed at the soft dirt of the opposite side of the ditch. It didn't take a Ph.D. in archaeology to recognize that she'd driven into an excavation trench.

Vindication shot through her. She'd been looking for an excavation she wasn't sure even existed. Just before the deer had dashed in front of her headlights, she'd seen a mound that could have been a buried Mayan ruin. It was at least five hundred yards away, which made the siting of this trench a little hard to figure, but there was no question about the excavation. At least this was proof she was on the right track.

In the right track, to be precise.

So now what? she asked herself as she pried her fingers off the steering wheel. She'd rented the Jeep, stocked up on supplies, bought four different maps, and driven some two hundred fifty miles on the strength of her determination not to be foiled by Jack Gibraltar. She wasn't going to be defeated by a three-foot ditch.

She could handle this, whether Jack Gibraltar thought so or not. She was a long way from a library, as her nemesis had so insufferably pointed out, but she *had* read the manual in the glove compartment of the Jeep. She knew how to put it into four-wheel drive. She probably couldn't do any worse than he had when he was driving her back from La Stela.

Well, all right. So maybe she could, she conceded a few moments later. Four-wheel drive, she discovered, gave all four wheels the opportunity to spin themselves deeper into the mud, at which point the engine sputtered, coughed once, and died.

Catherine took a deep breath, wiped her sweating hands on her chinos, and reassessed. She'd been in worse situations. A little more than twenty-four hours ago, for instance, she'd been in a bar in Chetumal frequented by smugglers, serious drinkers, and con men like Gibraltar.

Yes. And look where that got you, the inconvenient voice in her head informed her. She ignored it, shutting off the image of herself locked in Jack Gibraltar's arms, whispering in his ear while he told her whoppers in two languages.

After a few unsuccessful attempts at turning on the engine, she sat for a minute, thinking. The Jeep was equipped for emergencies: flares, two spare tires, a winch . . .

Feeling a lift of relief, Catherine reached for the radio. She'd read the manual for *that* too.

She hadn't just gone jaunting off on a miscalculated whim, she reassured herself. She'd decided she was going to find out the real truth about her aunt's scandal-laden codex. What she was doing was no more than Madrid would have done if their roles were reversed.

Oh, she was willing to admit she'd made some mistakes in dealing with Jack Gibraltar. Maybe he was a little out of her league. Too independent, too experienced, too . . . bilingual. But he'd sparked something in her that had fanned into life. Something she hadn't learned in a library.

She'd taken that spark with her when she left her aunt's apartment. She was on her own now.

And she was about to rescue herself by her own ingenuity. She took the radio's mike from its hook, turned on the radio, and spoke into it.

Static squawked back at her.

"Hello?" she tried again. "*Buenas noches?* Help?"

More static, and a faint, barely decipherable voice came back. But it was speaking English, and she managed to catch the frequency it was telling her to switch to.

"Okay," Catherine shouted into the mike. She fiddled with the dial and tuned in the new station. Her contact must be pretty far away—maybe back in the tiny village she'd passed before she turned onto this path—but he was there. With any luck the radio was in a vehicle equipped like hers, and the radio operator would be able to help her out.

The voice was marginally more recognizable after retuning. She gave her location and brief details, then added, "I'll need someone who knows how to work a winch with a good-sized four-wheel-drive vehicle, and I can pay for service if anyone can help me out here."

"Ten-four," the voice squawked, to her relief. "I'll find you."

Relief washed through her. The idea that she'd actually found some kind of road service in the middle of the jungle was too lucky to question. Winching her own Jeep out of the ditch might have been within her powers during daylight and with the manual propped open in front of her. It wasn't anything she was eager to try at night in the middle of a rain forest so thick she couldn't find a star anywhere above her. "I appreciate it," she said into the mike with heartfelt emotion.

"No prob. I won't be long."

"Thanks."

She got out of the Jeep, climbed up onto the edge of the ditch, and turned on her flashlight.

The beam illuminated a narrow opening through the dense greenery that bordered the twin ruts of the road beyond the trench. Fantastic shapes and patterns of leaves stirred in the moist air that whispered through the canopy of the rain forest. Above the rustling of the leaves was the steady, vibrant hum of thousands of insects—moths that flickered through the flashlight beam, giant winged beetles, familiar, whining mosquitoes. An exotic chorus of myriad chirps and whistles and calls evidenced the bird life in the canopy. Off to her right something howled.

Ten steps away from the Jeep took her far enough into the forest to give her a sense of being lost. Lost geographically, lost in time.

Awestruck, suddenly, by the heavy, thick blackness around her, Catherine played the beam of her flashlight down the road beyond the ditch, wondering if there were ruins there, perhaps not yet uncovered, that would yield secrets of a people who had tamed this jungle a thousand years ago, and then lost it again to the forces that covered their secrets and buried their treasures in its green depths.

Something howled again, a little closer than it had been, bringing her sharply back to the present. She didn't, Catherine acknowledged with reluctance that surprised her, know enough about the rain forest at night to be wandering around in it. Jack had mentioned that the natural life of the rain forest was not a threat. Field archaeologists faced it all the time. But she wasn't Madrid.

Not yet.

And the one man who seemed intent on keeping her in what he'd decided was her place was out of her life. She'd left him two hundred and fifty miles behind her.

She directed the flashlight beam here and there. Whether or not there were ruins at this site, it was obvious she wasn't going to be able to tell until daylight. She'd been feeling good about her luck. Maybe she'd better not push it.

She turned around, retraced her steps, climbed back into the Jeep, and waited to be rescued.

Just how unreliable her luck was became apparent soon after the rumble of an engine and the gleam of headlights announced her rescuer. She twisted around on the seat to stare at the truck pulling up behind her.

It was a Tracker.

Red. New. Familiar.

There had been, she realized angrily, something familiar about that static-distorted voice.

Something she should have recognized, even in English.

She clambered out of the Jeep and slammed the door at the same time he slammed the Tracker's. The doubled *thunk* reverberated in the hum of the night.

"What," she said in a voice that held no static whatever, "are you doing here?"

Gibraltar strolled toward the edge of the ditch, stopped there, and stood peering down in bland curiosity, hands hooked on his jeans pockets. "You called me," he said reasonably, as if the fact must have slipped her mind. "On the radio."

She had. The statement, though beside the point, was absolutely true. It might be the first indisputably true statement he'd made to her. And Catherine was a woman who *cared* about the truth.

But at the moment truth wasn't high on her list of priorities.

Catherine drew herself up ramrod straight. "I didn't call *you*," she said through her teeth. "I called anyone who was out there."

"I know." He grinned. "You got lucky."

Catherine controlled her tongue and fixed her gaze straight in front of her. It pinned him at about the level of his knees.

With a slow, involuntary sweep, Catherine's gaze followed the line of his pants up over his knees to where they smoothed against the masculine contours of his thighs. His weight was cocked on one hip, jeans pulled taut across his crotch and slung low on his hips. He wore no belt, and tucked into the loose waistband was a white dress shirt, dazzling in the Tracker's headlights, cuffs rolled up. His hands were propped on his hips, his tanned forearms showed glints of blond hair. He was wearing a tie, she noted, surprised. Unknotted, it draped around his neck under his open collar.

Two irrelevant thoughts drifted into her mind: one was the unlikely, unsettling, and, she had to admit, sexy image of Jack Gibraltar calling for her in a dress shirt and tie; the other was that next to his dress shirt and jeans, her suit would have looked stuffy.

Ridiculous, in fact. Almost as ridiculous as wrinkled chinos and muddy sneakers accessorized by a half-buried Jeep.

And one glance at his smug grin made her realize he was probably harboring exactly the same thoughts. Any moment now he'd express them in words that would undoubtedly include a reference to a library.

"You want to stand there in that mud puddle a little longer?" he asked amiably. "Or do you want a hand?" He placed one dry loafer on the edge of the trench and reached out toward her.

With a great deal of effort she unclenched her jaw, then, ignoring his hand, scrambled up by herself. Halfway up, she slipped and went down again. She was hauled up unceremoniously by her upper arms and deposited at the top of the ditch in front of him.

"You all right?"

Catherine wiped her hands on her muddy chinos and brushed her hair off her face with the back of one wrist. "Fine," she said shortly.

"Fine," he echoed, dropping his arms.

Even in her present mood, Catherine couldn't quite find a get-lost reply to that. He hadn't mentioned a library yet, she noticed. He hadn't even said anything untrue in the past three sentences. All he'd done was help her out of a ditch. His white dress shirt had muddy handprints at the elbows, where she'd automatically grasped him.

She grimaced, silencing her always overactive conscience. Why in God's name was he coming to her rescue, being so gallant when she had been trying so hard to get rid of him? She was supposed to have left him behind, dismissed by a definitive two-word note.

"Can you start her up?" he asked far too reasonably to give any opening to her simmering temper.

"No," she told him. "It will turn over, but it won't catch."

He crouched down on his haunches and peered under the rear wheels, then stood up again, facing her. "You probably pinched a fuel line. It will be dead weight being dragged out."

"Can you do it?"

"It will take some time."

"Some time?" Her stomach sank. She had to spend *some time* working with Jack Gibraltar?

Maybe she could walk back to the village. Surely it wouldn't take her much longer than the miserable drive.

"We'll pull that baby out in the morning."

"Morning?"

"Won't do any good to pull it out now. It will probably have to be towed, and there's no way I'm going to tow it over this road in the dark. I'll give you a ride back to town."

"Wait a minute," she said before he could turn around. He was doing it again—outmaneuvering her, coolly and effortlessly. And she was cooperating by letting her emotions override her logic. She drew herself up and started over. "You haven't answered my question, Mr. Gibraltar. What are you doing here?"

He gazed at her, eyebrows raised a little, blue gaze guileless. "That's easy, *querida*. I followed you."

She shut her eyes for a moment. She hated it when he called her Spanish endearments, she told herself. And she definitely did not feel a little shiver of pleasure work its way up her spine or her toes curl into the muddy soles of her sneakers. "Why?" she asked him.

"Well, for one thing"—he waited until she opened her eyes—"we had a date."

Catherine's conscience gave another inconvenient lurch. "I left you a note," she said with less determination than she'd meant.

He nodded. "I got it. *Dig—Campeche.*"

"Well, then—"

"Well, then, what? What kind of a note was that? *Dig—Campeche?* We were supposed to go out to dinner, lady. You stood me up!"

"I did not *stand you up*! I left you a note!"

"Oh?" He gestured vehemently enough to make his tie swing. "Well, I wouldn't have even seen it if I hadn't picked the lock on your aunt's door."

"So what?" she shot back. "I *knew* you'd get into my aunt's apartment. Why let something as arcane as the concept of privacy keep you from your appointed rounds?"

"The *concept of privacy*?" He took a step back, tipped his head to look at the nonvisible heavens, then faced her again, hands on his hips. "Tell me about the concept of privacy. Like why, all of a sudden, taking off for Campeche seemed like such a good idea?"

"Maybe I wanted to see where that codex came from!"

"Yeah? Campeche is a big place. You planning to cover every square inch of it?"

"No! Just the square inches you had on

your satellite scan when I called it up on my aunt's computer!"

In the taut, charged silence that followed her outburst, the small sounds of the tropical night filled the air, punctuated by another howl in the distance.

Catherine's huff of consternation was clearly audible. She hadn't really meant to bring up the subject of his computer. Especially not in the middle of the rain forest after dark when her only means of making a dignified exit was stuck in a ditch at her feet. She squeezed her eyes shut. "I can explain that," she muttered.

"*Querida,*" he said finally. There was an odd, rough note in his voice that made her open her eyes again.

"When you break into someone's computer," he said, smiling gently, "you're better off not trying to explain it."

"How . . . did you know?"

He shrugged. "There was a message on the board."

"I . . . don't suppose you want to tell me what that has to do with my aunt."

"Actually," Jack said, studying her for a moment with an unreadable expression on his face, "nothing."

She took another breath, got a last-minute

grasp on her unwound emotions, and shoved her muddy hands into her pockets. "Fine," she snapped out. "I'll fill in that information for myself."

"Yeah," he said, "you probably will." He didn't sound happy about it.

"I will," she told him. "As soon as I get out of this trench."

He covered his eyes with one hand, rubbing his temples, then looked at her. "Listen, Cathy. You don't need to get out of this trench."

She gritted her teeth against that feeling she got every time he called her Cathy. "Yes, I do," she said, challenging him. "How else am I going to get to my aunt's dig?"

He let out a long breath, then yanked his loose tie out from his collar. "I'll give you a ride to the damn dig if you want."

"What?"

"You want to go see the site on the map," he said again, "I'll take you there."

She frowned. "Why?"

"Why not? You really want to be driving around on an almost impassable road in the rain forest by yourself?"

She didn't, actually. The tropical forest she'd so blithely taken on in a rented Jeep with a few maps, one of them stolen, was way beyond her level of experience.

On the other hand, driving around Mexico after dark with Jack Gibraltar could be more dangerous than driving alone. The sparks between them were just too volatile to trust. She knew all about explosions. She'd studied basic physics.

Not to mention what she'd learned in the middle of her aunt's living room less than twenty-four hours ago.

"I don't make decisions on the basis of *why not*," she managed to say.

He started rubbing the back of his neck. "For someone whose long-range strategic plans can be stated as *Dig—Campeche*, you're splitting hairs, don't you think?"

"All right," she conceded. "Maybe my note didn't explain much, but—"

"But what? What do you think you're doing traipsing around the Yucatán, poking into some dig without the proper authorization?"

"Other people do it."

"Yeah. Lots of other people. Looters, locals who don't like them, locals who *do* like them . . . Lady, there are enough cops and robbers around these parts to make your average inner city neighborhood look tame."

It was an exaggeration.

She hoped.

She raised her chin. "Just tell me why this is your business, Mr. Gi—"

"Could you do me a favor, Cathy?" he cut in, his voice low and a little husky. "Since I just drove several hundred miles to keep a date, and since I just offered you a guided tour to the territory you discovered by breaking into my computer, and since I'm about to get you pulled out of this ditch you got yourself into, do you think you could call me Jack?"

"I . . ." *No. She couldn't.* If she called him Jack, she'd start thinking that she could trust him. That he'd given in on something. That he was treating her somehow . . . honorably. She'd start thinking she liked him, maybe.

"Listen, Cathy," he went on in that voice that stirred her newly discovered impulses, "you left me a note which I don't want to have to explain to your aunt in case she gets back before you do."

She frowned. "What do you mean? Are you expecting her back soon?"

"No," he muttered, exasperated. "Or you either, considering your lack of a game plan."

So she didn't have detailed strategic plans, she thought defiantly. She was new at this business. She hadn't done a lot of computer break-ins or midnight runs through the rain forest of Mexico. She'd learn. He'd sparked a few more of those reckless, un-Catherinelike urges, and she wasn't, by God, going back to her library!

"Then that leaves only one question unanswered," she snapped back at him. "Why should I *let* you rescue me from my nonstrategic plans?"

He assessed her in the headlights of his Tracker, idly stuffing the tie into his pocket, while wheels turned in his head. She could *feel* him coming to some kind of conclusion about just what he could use to get to her.

Slowly, his lips turned up in a grin.

Catherine took a deep breath. Something had changed between them, she thought. Something that gave her a heady feeling that this was no longer a con game with her as the victim. She had become a co-conspirator with him in a game of wits and challenge and whispered Spanish in the dark. That recklessness that Jack Gibraltar had awakened started buzzing in the pit of her stomach and the base of her spine, and everyplace else capable of sending tiny pulses of excitement racing along her nerve endings.

She knew already what his offer would be.

"Because," he said finally, "I can tell you what *South Five* means."

SEVEN

The small cantina hotel in the tiny backwater village of Taxtican, which should have rolled up its awnings at sunset, was improbably noisy, uncharacteristically well lit, and musical. A knot of laughing, drinking wedding guests milled around outside the single entrance as Jack pulled up to the curb and shut off the engine. Clearly this was the best place in town to have a party. It was also, Jack happened to know, the only place in a couple million acres of rain forest.

He glanced across the seat at his silent passenger, considering his options in light of their credibility.

Not great, he concluded. The Crusader on a Mission who'd just made a minor deal with the devil himself wasn't going to buy any glib, facile *vive l'amour* explanation about the hotel being booked up with amorous guests and not having extra rooms. He was going to have to tell her the truth.

It was getting to be a bad habit.

She glanced at him quizzically when he made no move to get out of the Tracker.

"Cathy," he said, touching his thumb and forefinger to his temples, "we've got a small problem here."

"Oh?"

He dropped his hand to look at her. The wide, wary brown eyes were as easy to read as an open codex. Despite their deal, or maybe because of it, her distrust had returned in spades, and it didn't take a computer scientist to figure out that the object of it was sitting beside her in the driver's seat.

"The problem," Jack said decisively and, he hoped, convincingly, "is Blasquo."

"Blasquo?" She frowned in puzzlement. "Why is Blasquo a problem?"

"Think about it without all the ivory-tower niceties. The man thinks he was scammed by Madrid and yours truly."

"I know."

He shot her a frown.

"I've figured out that much by myself."

Jack gave her another long look, evaluating her ability to take in an unlikely situation—and not come to too many correct conclusions. This would be a hell of a lot easier, he thought not for the first time, if Catherine Moore were a little less good at thinking.

"Yes. Well. The point is, the man has a suspicious mind."

She raised an eyebrow.

Blasquo wasn't the only one with a suspicious mind, Jack reflected grimly. "The man isn't happy about *you and me*, Cathy," he said, spelling it out. "He isn't sure our . . . ah . . . association . . . is purely social. He was especially unhappy when I blew off the dinner engagement. I had to give him an excuse."

"What did you tell him?"

Jack's mouth quirked at one corner. "Told him I had a hot chance for an earth-moving connection with a woman who wouldn't take no for an answer."

The brown eyes widened as she took in the implications of that statement. "Hot chance? A woman who wouldn't take—"

"That's right, Cath. You."

"Me?" The word rose into a squeak. "You mean you actually implied—"

"I tried my best to imply it. And with the

help of that getup you were wearing in La Stela, maybe I succeeded."

She blinked, a gesture that managed to convey outrage, incredulity, and shock. She was beginning to get the point, Jack decided, and she didn't like it.

"Get the ivy out of your eyes, babe," Jack told her. "Blasquo knows everyone from Chetumal to Villahermosa. He'll hear about anything that goes on. And what I want him to hear is hot nights, steamy sex, and no time for diversions like checking out Mayan codices, because Mr. Blasquo would not be happy if he thought you and I were driving around Yucatán conducting business."

"Suspicions? Spying? Reports? That's absolutely crazy! And even if you think someone does suspect something, you have no right to tell—"

"Not only tell it," he interrupted her, "show it. We're going to put on one hell of an act."

"What are you talking about?" She shook her head and started again. "What makes you think I'd go along with that kind of arrangement? What makes *me* think I should even believe all this? How do I know you're not the one with the overly suspicious mind?"

His mouth quirked again. "Are you fond of your career, Professor?"

She stared at him, silenced.

"I thought so." He pinned her with a steady gaze. "This is the way it is, unless you want to bet your career I'm wrong. Not to mention your sweet neck."

"Oh, really—"

"We're going to be lovers, Cathy. We share a room, we share a vehicle, and as long as we're in any kind of public place where Blasquo can conceivably get a report of it, we're locked together like squash blossoms on a vine. Got it?"

She shut her mouth abruptly, but Jack could sense the thoughts churning in her head—this hadn't been part of their deal. Neither had the information about Blasquo, which she didn't quite believe and was not quite experienced enough to process. Fortunately. But the Crusader on a Mission was caught on the sharp prongs of what she was willing to allow in exchange for finding out what she wanted to know.

"The rules have changed, Cathy," he said softly, almost sympathetically.

"What?"

"They changed when you broke into my

computer and decided to take off for parts unknown. Like Alice down the rabbit hole, you know? It's not all that easy to go back."

"I don't know what you—" She stopped, unable to bring herself to deny his charge.

There was something a little too vulnerable about her honesty. She was no fool, Jack realized. She knew damn well what was going on between the two of them even if she didn't know squat about why the hell they'd gotten tangled up in the first place.

When she'd climbed into his truck and he'd tossed her gear in the back, the physical tension between them had taken an upward leap. She wasn't quite the respectable, responsible college professor anymore. She was a woman who'd broken into his computer, taken off alone into the rain forest, and then agreed to some unholy deal with a man she didn't trust, and the idea scared the hell out of her.

It ought to. It scared the hell out of him too.

"Jack," she said, worried.

"Yeah?"

"Maybe we could just . . . register under different names?"

He sighed, pinching the bridge of his nose

between thumb and forefinger. "Lady, you couldn't even break into my computer without confessing to it three minutes after you saw me. Let's keep this act simple, okay?"

"*Simple?*"

"As in *workable.* I'm not any happier about this than you are, but that's the deal. For better or for worse, we're stuck with each other."

She grimaced. "As in marriage?"

"Yeah." He gave her a long, hooded look. "Except that when we get the divorce there won't be anything to fight about."

There was a short, evaluative silence, then she said softly, "There's always something to fight about. Sometimes innocent parties get caught in the crossfire."

He gave her a sharp look.

"Ace told me about your parents," she said.

Disbelief and annoyance came out as a short, wordless huff. Jack pressed the heel of his hand against the steering wheel and swore a blue streak in silence. "Ace was a regular gold mine of information, wasn't he?"

"He admires you. He likes to talk about you."

"Ace would admire anybody who knew computers."

"Or anybody who took the time to lecture him and then befriend him after he broke into your truck?"

He slanted her a sarcastic look. "Maybe I have hauled him into the local police station. It might have kept his mouth shut, at least."

"That's not your style, according to Ace."

"That's not my style?"

She shook her head. "No. Your style is protecting Ace from his own folly . . ."

"Listen, Cathy."

" . . . giving a hand to all those kids who might be headed down the wrong path."

Jack leaned his head back against the seat and closed his eyes. "Just repaying a debt. Like Ace probably told you, I've gone straight."

"I think it's more than a debt. I think you care about those kids."

He turned his head toward her. The brown eyes were watching him steadily with curiosity and concern, but no hint of censure. There was a softness in the look that pulled at something deep in his gut and shocked him down to the soles of his feet. He wanted to talk to her. Tell her how it had been. Tell her how he *felt*, for God's sake.

He forced the urge aside. Wanting her

warm and willing and whispering in Spanish was dangerous enough, but wanting her to care? It wasn't even sane.

So why the hell did he?

"Don't get the idea that I'm some kind of hero. I caught a bunch of kids trying to break into my truck. It was in my own interest to give them something else to do."

"You could have turned them in."

"Yeah, well, sometimes traditional authority isn't the quickest route to justice."

She was frowning, giving him a look of dangerous curiosity and even more dangerous concern. "You *have* gone straight, haven't you?" she said slowly. "You weren't just saving your neck when you made that announcement about the codex that made my aunt look guilty."

He looked away from her, covering his eyes with one hand. "Dammit all to hell, Cathy."

"What?" she said.

He dropped his hand. There wasn't any safe way to answer that question. Therefore it wasn't going to get answered. Period.

"Listen," he said. "Let's keep this simple, okay? We're going to spend the night in this hotel here, and we're running a little act for the benefit of a man with a suspicious mind and lots of contacts. It's covering both our tails. Keep that in mind. You and me, simple cover story, minor con game. Got it?"

"That's hardly the whole story."

"That's all you can handle. Don't screw it up."

She flinched, just enough to make Jack realize he'd hurt her. Regret knifed through him, setting off a warning he shouldn't have needed. He didn't have any choice. He couldn't level with her. When the hell had a necessary decision gotten so personal?

"Your trust in me is inspiring, Mr. Gibraltar," she muttered, covering the hurt with sarcasm.

"*Jack.*"

"I beg your pardon?"

"Call me Jack, *querida*. We're lovers."

"How could I possibly have forgotten that fact?"

Jack noted the flare of anger across her cheeks and welcomed it. At least it replaced the wounded look in her eyes. And sparring with her was a hell of a lot safer than what they'd gotten into a moment ago.

"If you need a reminder, *querida*—"

"I don't!" she said too quickly. "I'm going along with this . . . *con game* . . . because it *might* be a necessary charade. I don't need any reminders beyond that."

He nodded. But the thought had crossed her mind. Before, during, or after the discussion of his personal history? "Fine," he said. "As long as you stash the suede skirts and keep your blouses mostly on your body, I shouldn't have any trouble keeping the signals straight."

"Fine!" she snapped.

"Fine." He met her gaze across the seat. "I'll go rent us a room."

She swallowed that with a little effort. "All right."

"We'll go directly to the room, sleep late tomorrow, act like we don't know anyone else exists, and call in for room service if you're hungry."

"Do I leave my suede skirt draped over the bedpost," she gritted, "for the benefit of the room service waiter?"

"It'd be a nice touch. We're going for an Academy Award here."

"So I gather."

"Can you do it?"

She glared at him, offended by his blunt question of her competence. More than offended, he noted. Seething. "Yes."

"Good." He glanced toward the wedding

guests outside the restaurant door, some of whom were watching them with idle curiosity, then he reached across the seat, caught her by the back of the neck, and pulled her toward him. "First act," he murmured, and brought his mouth down on hers.

She made a sound of surprise as his lips slanted and pressed against hers, demanding a lover's access. His fingers twined into the thick, tangled hair at the back of her neck, and he felt the heat of her hand against his shoulder, then her lips opened to the demanding penetration of his tongue.

Blood running thick and hot in his veins, Jack claimed her mouth with sudden urgency, and he realized her gasp of surprise had sounded far more elemental, far too raw for any pretense.

He pulled back from her and reached for the door handle in one savage motion, let himself out of the Tracker, and slammed the door behind him hard enough to raise heads and elicit murmurs from the crowd around the door.

What the hell was he doing kissing her like that?

More to the point, what the hell did he think he was doing? He had the upper hand in this game, but he didn't need to be reminded of how fast that could change.

Particularly in a shared hotel room. Particularly with the kind of heat they generated on instantaneous contact. Despite the fact that she'd broken into his computer network.

Because of the fact she'd broken into his computer network.

Catherine Moore, Crusader, was just a little too dangerous to handle.

He'd damn well better remember that he was supposed to be the infidel.

He got a blunt reminder when he rounded the corner of the doorway and glanced across the small parking lot.

A familiar white convertible stood in the last row.

EIGHT

By the time Jack had taken care of their registration, parked the truck, and retrieved their bags, Catherine had managed to convince herself she hadn't just handed over the whole game to a con man who could set her on fire with a single candy-from-a-baby kiss.

But she hadn't exactly seized control of the situation either, she decided grimly, following him up the outside staircase and along a balcony walkway to Room 14. Instantaneous, thorough combustion from one hot kiss did not constitute seizing control. And objecting after the fact would make her feel like more of a fool than she already did for responding to him so thoroughly.

If he hadn't been so damn convinced she couldn't pull this off, if he hadn't intimated that she wasn't *capable* of brazening out a con game, she wouldn't have kissed him back.

Might not have anyway.

All right, she admitted, she probably would have. She didn't seem to have any resistance to him at all. If she'd been an ancient Mayan, Jack Gibraltar would have been smallpox.

And getting involved with him would be just as disastrous. He'd already made her his partner in crime. Every time he touched her she was one step closer to becoming his partner in . . . earth moving.

It wasn't her thing, Catherine told herself firmly. It was just that he made her feel reckless and furious and daring and determined. He made her feel entirely too much.

He was the kind of man she could get terribly attached to, the kind of man it would be ruinous to get attached to.

Jack dropped their bags on the walkway outside their door, which he then unlocked and pushed open. Catherine followed him inside.

"Well, here it is," he said. "Privacy."

She glanced around. *Privacy* consisted of wooden floors, white stuccoed walls, bright woven rugs, and, in the center of the room, as if the decorators had been afraid it would be overlooked, one double bed.

"Privacy," she echoed, folding her arms in front of her, then unfolding them again. She was not going to mention the bed. She wasn't going to open any subjects that had anything to do with beds. Let Jack Gibraltar bring up their sleeping arrangement if he was concerned about it.

Apparently he wasn't. He crossed to the bathroom, glanced into it, then made a sound of approval and stepped back.

When he glanced toward her, she unstuck her feet and inched a little farther away from the bed. Dammit, hadn't he noticed there was only one?

"If you've got a black negligee in your suitcase, now's the time to get it out."

"I don't."

Hands on his hips, he considered her, apparently displeased she hadn't brought a wardrobe of black lace with her.

Feeling irrationally insulted, Catherine recrossed her arms and glared at him. "Why don't you just get out your satin boxer shorts and leave it at that?"

"Haven't got any," he muttered. "I don't wear shorts."

"You don't—" She shut her mouth abruptly, appalled at the betraying sensation of heat creeping into her face. Leave it to a man who didn't wear shorts to bring up the subject of underwear. She glanced back at him. *What did he sleep in?*

"Don't worry about it, *querida*," he said as if he'd read her mind. "I don't wear negligees either."

"I wasn't *worried* about it," she said stiffly. "As a matter of fact, I'd hardly given it a thought."

He stared at her a moment, mouth quirked, then crossed the room to the bed and muttered, "Good. You think too much anyway."

"I'll work on breaking the habit."

"I don't think you can help it. It's a professional failing."

Catherine bit down on her temper and, jaw clenched, reminded herself of her reasons for being there. She'd come to find out about her aunt. She'd practically sold her soul to get some answers out of him, and he wasn't living up to his end of the deal. "And just what are the professional requirements for *your* line of work, Mr. Gibraltar? Besides a supply of black lace and a few transparent computer codes?"

He started to lean down to pick up his duffel bag, but then straightened and turned toward her. "You want to talk about this?"

She met his gaze, chin up. "About what 'South Five' means?"

His gaze softened a little. Just enough to do something to her insides. "About you and me, Cathy," he said, "here and now, for the night."

She raised her chin a little higher, aware that her heart was pounding in a way that could have been an early symptom of . . . smallpox, maybe. She couldn't let that happen. "What's to talk about?" she said.

He gave her another long, disbelieving look, then let out a breath. "Have it your way. You want the first shower?"

She shrugged elaborately. "Go ahead." She wasn't even sure she'd packed a robe. She'd left in a hurry, before her newfound impulse toward reckless bravery could desert her.

"You sure?" He frowned at her, then picked up his duffel bag and swung it onto the bed. He rummaged in one of the zippered compartments and came up with a towel and a bottle of shampoo. "Okay, then." He unbuttoned his shirt, one-handed, and shrugged out of it.

For the life of her, Catherine couldn't help but stare at the bare male chest above the loose-waisted jeans.

He didn't apparently care that he was undressing while she watched. His hands went to his waist, and her pulse leapt with the realization that she had no idea how far Jack Gibraltar would go and consider it normal.

Would he take off all his clothes in front of her and wander into the bathroom naked? Images paraded themselves in front of her mind. They were about as cool as hot molten lava.

But he merely hitched up his jeans and toed off his shoes. While her undisciplined gaze took in his half-clothed body with fascination, a feeling suspiciously and unacceptably like disappointment cooled the gathering heat in Catherine's stomach.

Lips pursed in a silent whistle, he strode into the bathroom, then the door shut behind him.

With a small creak it opened again, like the lid on her errant fantasies. She glanced over her shoulder as he slammed the door with a little more force. This time it latched, but fifteen seconds later she heard the same creak.

He shut it again.

Hypnotized, Catherine stared at the door,

while behind it Jack Gibraltar unsnapped and unzipped his jeans and stepped out of them, probably pulling down his underwear in the same gesture. He would lean down to snag the shampoo, then pull the shower door closed, all the while moving with the easy, athletic certainty that was too blatantly sexual to be described as grace.

The latch held just until she heard the sound of the shower hitting the stall, then the door eased open again.

A cloud of moisture drifted out of the bathroom, scented with soap and water and laden with imagined pictures that were steaming her up like a bathroom mirror.

Catherine let the breath out of her constricted lungs, and acknowledged the unmistakable fact that Jack Gibraltar excited her in a way she'd never expected to be by any man. He'd kissed her in the parking lot as if he had every right to eclipse her common sense and play chicken with her fragile bravado. And she'd kissed him back because she was fascinated by his daring and his arrogance and his outrageous lack of decorum, and because she wanted more of him than a shared con game and a pretend kiss.

She wanted more from him.

More honesty, more information, more . . . trust.

Dammit all to hell, he'd said when she ventured a guess about the way he seemed to have sold out her aunt. He hadn't wanted to tell her whether or not he was letting Madrid take the rap for him.

Why? Because he was guilty?

Or because he wasn't?

And if he *hadn't* sold out her aunt, then maybe he was someone she could . . .

Could what?

Catherine's mouth curved in a faint smile that fixed itself, for a long while, on the half-open bathroom door. The answers that were running through her mind were definitely not repeatable.

The water in the shower stopped, and she heard the click of the latch on the stall. She waited, breath held, for him to shut the bathroom door, but it stayed ajar. Through the crack she caught a glimpse of skin—wet, tanned, with a darker shadow at hip level when he turned—and her heart began to thud again, accompanied by Jack's nonchalant and unknowing whistle.

She turned her head around just as he walked out, his hair wet and dripping, shirtless, and crossed to the bed. He was wearing his jeans, zipped, not snapped, slung low on his lean hips, exposing a wide, muscled chest swirled with blond hair.

She glanced away when he looked at her. "I think I left you enough hot water," he said, frowning at her in a way she couldn't read.

"Thanks," she said with a squeak. She cleared her throat and tried again. "Thanks."

"Don't thank me yet. You haven't taken the shower."

"Yes. Well, I . . ."

He opened his mouth to say something, then apparently thought better of it. He reached down for her overnight bag, heaved it up onto the bed. The overstrained catch gave with a small, resonant *ping*, and the contents exploded as the top flew open.

"Oh, I should have warned you about the—"

He scowled at her, then shook a pair of lace-trimmed black panties off his wrist and stepped back as if the suitcase had attacked him.

"—catch," she finished.

"Right," Jack muttered.

Ignoring the color she felt in her face, Catherine gathered a change of underwear and an oversize T-shirt that would have to double as a nightgown and toted the lot to the bathroom. She shut the door and made sure it latched.

Jack stared at the door for a moment, then turned back to the uncontested bed. "What's to talk about?" he muttered with sarcasm.

He was walking a high wire over the Sarlac Pit with a partner who was quite possibly the worst liar in North America, and she was trying to dissemble her way out of a sexual situation so hot it could melt the wire.

It was, he reflected, a hell of a way to run a con game.

One bed. One cruising shark. One smart, sexy distraction who made sounds in the back of her throat that made him think with his gonads instead of his head.

Whatever the hell she'd done to him, it could not be classified as read-only-memory. If he didn't watch himself, he'd end up with the entire contents of his brain reformatted.

And Professor Catherine Moore, Ph.D., with a few recently acquired credentials in larceny, didn't want to talk about it.

She came out of the bathroom five minutes later wearing a white cotton T-shirt that looked as if it had been designed for the Colossus of Rhodes. She was obviously, he decided with irritation, sending him a message he couldn't have missed even if he were three days dead.

"That's the closest thing you've got to a negligee?" he asked her, snatching his duffel bag and dropping it onto the floor.

She glanced down at her T-shirt and gave him a disdainful look. "Use your imagination, Mr. Gibraltar. I have a feeling that's what's most at work here anyway."

"It's a toss-up. I'll give you that," he muttered.

"What?"

"If my imagination was the only thing going on here, believe me, you wouldn't need any props, but that's not the point of this maneuver." He pinned her with a glare. "You might want to remember that, if your own imagination isn't too stressed."

"Meaning what?" she asked.

Her quick swallow made Jack wonder just what was occupying her imagination. He let himself smile through gritted teeth. She may not want to talk about it, but it had been more than a passing thought in her mind.

One bed. One cruising shark. One lousy liar.

"Meaning," Jack said carefully, "a smart woman would assume that Blasquo is watching us like a hawk—or having someone do it for him. And we need all the props we can get."

She shrugged, crossed to her suitcase, then glanced casually toward the door.

"And don't even think about going to get the sleeping bag, *querida*."

She spun around toward him. "I don't see why—"

"What were you planning to do—walk through the lobby with it on the way to our lovers' tryst?"

"I wasn't—"

"Of course, you could put it under that T-shirt, but you'd look like you were ready to deliver any minute."

"Don't you think that's a little—"

"What?"

She took a breath—not much of one, but enough to let him know just what she was wearing under the oversize shirt—nothing. "I have to tell you I'm not convinced this is really necessary."

That was the problem, all right. And he couldn't tell her just how necessary it was. She'd want to know too many unexplainable details. Frustrated, he leaned down to his bag and yanked out a shirt. "You don't have to be convinced. You're not here following your instincts. We have a deal."

"Which you haven't, so far, lived up to."

He straightened, weight slung on one hip, thumbs hooked into his pockets. "All right. What do you want to know?"

Her eyes flicked, just briefly, to the unsnapped waistband of his jeans, and he thought for one intensely interesting moment that she was going to forget the question.

She didn't. "I want to know what South Five means."

"Why?"

"*Why?*"

"Yeah. What are you planning to do with the information? Run it through the university computers? Use it to track down your aunt's latest dig? Mention it to Blasquo and get yourself up to your sweet neck in the same kind of trouble you were looking for at La Stela?"

Her jaw clenched, but she said evenly enough, "I'm not looking for trouble. I'm looking for information."

He shook his head. "In this game, lady, information *is* trouble. It's not a library, dammit!"

"I know that!" she snapped back at him.

"If I wanted a library, I would have stayed home!"

She propped her hands on her hips, and the tentlike shirt pulled taut across her breasts. He could see the faint rise and fall of her breathing as she leaned toward him, furious.

She was right, he realized. She was no librarian. She might be naive and inexperienced, but she had stubbornly taken the first step down a road that definitely didn't lead to a library, and she wasn't likely to step back.

Not if he had anything to say about it.

The thought made him frown. Dammit, his plan as to how to deal with her had been simple and straightforward. He'd tell her just what he had to, no more, keep her out of trouble for as long as necessary, then send her back where she belonged.

If he still knew where that was when this game was over.

If he still knew his own name, for God's sake.

"I think you're right about that, Cath," he said slowly, watching her. "You weren't meant for a library."

She blinked, disarmed by a comment she clearly hadn't expected. She stared at him, looking for the catch in what he'd just told her.

"Listen," he said before she could ask him what he meant. "I want you to get something clear, now. Maybe you could sell Blasquo on the idea of South Five being important, but, believe me, you don't want to get mixed up with him."

"I wouldn't sell you out, Jack," she said slowly. "We have a deal."

Jack recognized the truthfulness of her words, then shut his eyes and muttered a silent epithet. Something that was too close to guilt sliced through him. God, what was it about this woman that made him feel as if he ought to be cut into small pieces and fed to Archie?

He was doing what he had to do. And if he didn't find some way to handle what she did to him, he wouldn't *need* to worry about her getting them all hung. They'd *all* be fed to Archie.

"All right," he conceded when both of them had held the silence too long. "We have a deal." He rubbed the back of his neck, where Cathy's effect on him was knotting his muscles.

"So what does South Five mean?"

"It's shorthand. Directions on a dig. For the excavation."

"*Madrid's* last excavation?"

He hesitated a little too long, considering, before he said, "Yeah."

"There's more, isn't there?"

"Yeah. And I'm not telling you, Cath. You don't need to know it."

She made a sound of shocked disbelief. "*I don't need to know it?*"

"The less you know, the less chance there is that Blasquo will get to you."

"What if he does? I told you—I won't sell you out."

"Dammit, Cath! If Blasquo gets to you, you'd better be prepared to sell me out. Me and anyone you need to, to save your neck. Because that's exactly what everyone else mixed up in this deal will do."

She uttered a word explicit enough to raise his eyebrows.

"Cath—"

"I don't believe that! *Everyone* else? Who? Me? My aunt? You?"

"Let's just leave it at you for now, all right? Because if you're not willing to devote yourself to saving your own tail, you don't belong here."

"That's for me to decide!"

"Not if you don't know what you're doing."

"I know I'm sick of someone else telling me where I belong on the basis of information *I don't need to know.*"

"That was the attitude that got you into trouble at La Stela, *querida.*"

"I don't recall being in trouble at La Stela," she snapped back at him.

"Maybe not, but you sure as hell had one interested customer when I picked you up out front."

"My customer?"

"Yeah. The one who followed you home. Remember him?"

"How do you know he was following me? You're the one with the secret mi—"

Jack cut off her full-scale outrage with a sharp gesture of his hand. Outside the room, heavy footsteps were taking the stairs, pausing at the top, as if getting bearings, then starting down the outside corridor.

"What are you—"

Jack took a step toward her, spun her around toward the door with her back to his chest, and brought his mouth down onto the side of her neck.

She made some shocked, astonished sound, and started to bring her arms back to push him away. He caught her hands in one of his and held them trapped between the small of her back and his hard stomach.

"Easy, *querida*," he murmured just beneath her ear, moving his lips against her skin. "Trust me on this one." His words drew another incoherent protest from her. He ignored it, catching her hair and tugging just hard enough to tip her head back against his shoulder, coaxing her head to the side to give his mouth access to the exposed cord of her neck.

Her breath rushed out, then she leaned back against him.

"Good girl," he murmured.

Her back arched slightly, in the most subtle of responses, but Jack felt his own reaction sizzle down his chest and stomach straight to the core of this rough intimacy, where the zipper of his jeans pressed against her backside.

He thought what they were doing was more dangerous than any threat walking down that outside hall. Then a key rattled in the lock, the door to the room swung open, and a man carrying a tray full of drinks poked his head around it.

Catherine uttered a single undecipherable

word. Jack's arm clamped more tightly around her, then he snapped his chin up and stared in apparent surprise at the intruder.

The man gave them a swift once-over, raised an eyebrow, then smiled in apology. "*Lo siento.* I must have the wrong room." He backed out, closing the door behind him.

Jack let her go.

Still reeling from surprise, Catherine turned around to face him, her mouth opened for a question she hadn't formed yet. He put two fingers against her lips, turned his head to listen to the footsteps retreating uncertainly from the door, then met her gaze, his eyes dark, and walked her backward toward the bed.

The mattress came up against the back of her knees. "What—?"

He gave her a gentle push and she went down, catching herself on her elbows as the mattress creaked. Jack followed her, leaning over her until his mouth nuzzled her ear.

She hitched herself up on the bed, away from him. The springs creaked. Jack slid his hand under her shoulder and eased her back down. "Stay here, Cathy," he murmured close to her ear.

"What's going on?"

Jack let out a breath. "You do have a way of phrasing things, *querida*." His leg covered one of hers, his thigh was wedged into the V where her T-shirt was pulled up between her legs, and his hips were in full contact with her body so that she had to know what the hell was going on under his zipper.

"That man . . ."

"Room service," Jack muttered.

Her eyes searched his. Their pupils were so dilated, they looked dark enough to hold any truth she'd ever denied. Dark enough to see the ones he, too, had denied. "Jack," she said, her voice husky. "I don't think—"

"Don't think, Cathy. For once, all right?"

She wiggled, easing herself away from him again. Jack put his hand on her rib cage, holding her still.

"But when we got the room, when you said, out in the parking lot—"

"Dammit, I thought you didn't want to talk about it!"

"That was different. I didn't want to talk about . . ." She trailed off, then closed her eyes, and her throat worked as she swallowed.

This was exactly what she hadn't wanted to talk about, Jack knew. The heat, the quivering catch of breath, the swift, ready desires that spiraled between them in a barely controlled nuclear reaction headed straight for meltdown.

If he moved his thumb just another inch, he knew he'd feel her heartbeat, quickened and restless and demanding—a match for his.

"Jack?"

"Yeah?"

"Is that man coming back?"

"I think we can count on it, Cathy. Since he didn't have the wrong room."

Her hands were pressed against the mattress behind her, her weight propped on her elbows. The T-shirt molded her unconfined breasts. She swallowed again. "So we're supposed to just . . . wait for him?"

Protective instinct rose sharply in him. She was too damn vulnerable. For her good. For his. And too damn dangerous to his emotions.

When he'd kissed her in the parking lot, her sweet, sensuous mouth had pulled him deep into his own nature to a place that was warm, private, and marked by her taste, her scent, her presence. He'd wanted to keep going deeper into it, with her sounds in his ears and his hands all over her body, making her sigh, making her whisper, making her beg for more.

He'd been there with other women. But none of them had brought his body to maximum heat as Cathy did—with a single incoherent sound and a sweet, open-mouthed kiss.

Now, as she met his gaze, a slow fire started burning in him, a reaction that went beyond the physical.

His thumb had started a slow, sensual caress, rubbing the soft material of her T-shirt just below her breast. He glanced down and saw the outline of a taut nipple.

Jack flattened his hand against her ribs, absorbing the heat of her skin through his palm, pulling the fabric tight over her engorged nipple.

She made a sound in the back of her throat.

"Don't do that, Cathy."

"Don't do what?" she asked, her eyes languid with sensuality.

"Make that sound. Because if you do, I'm going to kiss you."

Slowly, her mouth softened. "I thought you might."

"Do you want me to?" he murmured.

"Oh, yes. *Sí.*"

He leaned over her, bending his back until his mouth was an inch from her breast. His hand cupped the soft swell and his other hand slid up to tangle in her hair and tug gently until she let her head tip back and she arched a little higher toward his mouth.

He lowered his head the last fraction of an inch, opened his lips, and gently, with exquisite care, closed his teeth over the crest.

"Jack . . ."

His name was a soft, breathless cry that went through him like the heat of a sun-baked desert, like the heat of her hands suddenly grasping his shoulders.

His hand trailed down to the hem of her T-shirt, then slid underneath it and up the length of her thigh.

"Wait." She moved to cover his hand.

He pulled back, searching her face. "What?" he said, his voice gruff.

Her face was flushed and he could feel the rushed cadence of her breathing. "What?" he said, more demanding.

"I don't want that man to walk in again."

Jack swore softly, then drew his hand back and smoothed the T-shirt down to cover her bare leg. It wasn't likely, he thought, that Blasquo's crony would walk in again without knocking, but he didn't want to take the chance. The need to protect her surged again.

Con game or no con game, common sense or lack of it, he wasn't going to let Cathy be seen in any act more compromising than kissing.

Belatedly, he became aware of what he was actually thinking. He moved away from her, sliding his hand up her arm to her shoulder, swearing again.

She didn't say anything, but ambivalence lapped in her expression and cooled the growing passion he'd stirred in her eyes. His hand tightened on her shoulder.

"That man wasn't room service."

"No."

"He was the one who approached me outside La Stela."

Jack nodded. "Blasquo's man. He must have . . . followed you, Cath. In a white convertible. I recognized it out in the lot."

"But what would he want? What would Blasquo want with us? The map? The satellite scan I got from your computer?"

"I don't think so."

"Why not?"

"Ah . . . Cathy. Listen. It's an old dig."

She didn't move away from him, but she did ask, "How old?"

"How old?" he repeated. One corner of

his mouth quirked up. Damn good question. "That's . . . not easy to say," he hedged.

"We had a deal, Jack," she said. "You were going to tell the truth."

Well, not exactly. Absolute truth hadn't been part of the deal. But, dammit, he didn't really want to lie to her either.

So just tell her, Gibraltar. The map she saw is two months old.

Then cut to the chase. Or the capture, to put it accurately.

The luminous brown eyes gazed at him without wavering, but her lips trembled just a little with uncertainty. "Cathy." His voice sounded as thick as that damn mud under the wheels of her Jeep. "What do you say you just trust me on this one?"

She wanted to. He could see it in the way her eyes dropped from his, the way her breath caught. And damn if that didn't make him feel worthless.

He knew he was going to regret saying it, but he said it anyway. "Two months."

"Two months."

He let go of her, rolled onto his back, and draped his wrist over his eyes. "The satellite scan—it's two months old."

"And what does the Five in South Five mean?"

"Five hundred meters."

"Five hundred *meters*?" The mattress creaked as she levered herself up on one elbow. "That's the trench I got the Jeep stuck in! Isn't it?"

He glanced toward her, the back of his wrist still resting on the bridge of his nose. "Yeah, I imagine it is."

"My aunt *dug* that trench!"

"Could have," Jack said cautiously, but he might as well not have spoken for all the good it did in tamping down the spark of discovery that was creeping into her voice.

"And you let me just walk away from it!"

"It was pitch dark. What do you think you were going to see?"

"Nothing, if you had your way about it, would I?"

She'd sat up and was staring down at him as if she'd just discovered he was using the Holy Grail to brush his teeth in. Jack raised himself on his elbow. "For God's sake, you don't even know for sure it was Madrid's trench. And even if it was—"

"Is," she said.

"Huh?"

"Maybe it *is* her trench. Maybe it's still active."

He sat up the rest of the way and rubbed the back of his neck. "Oh, I don't—"

She swung her legs over the edge of the bed and pushed herself to her feet. "I *know* my aunt's not on the Mexican Riviera," she stated, pacing across the room. "That's why no one's heard from her."

"Cathy . . ."

"That's why no one knows where she is. She's here."

He rubbed the back of his neck again. "Yeah."

She turned around and paced back toward him. "I bet that's what she's been doing."

"Cathy, I don't—"

"It has to be! It's just too much of a coincidence to be anything else."

Well, not exactly, he thought.

"Don't even try to tell me I'm wrong about this," she said, finally looking at him. "I should have known it from the beginning!"

No, he decided, looking at her flushed cheeks and the determined spark in her brown eyes. He couldn't tell her she was wrong.

But he couldn't tell her anything else either.

Dammit, he knew what she'd do with the truth. She wouldn't pack up and go home.

She'd dive straight into the sharks and count on making honest deals with them. And he wouldn't bet a used peso any of them would come out intact.

She circled the foot of the bed, then leaned over to pull her suitcase toward her. She began stuffing clothes into it.

"What are you doing, Cath?"

"I'm going back there."

"*Now?*"

"Yes. Now." She selected a split skirt and stepped into it.

"Are you nuts? You can't go there now."

"Watch me." She slipped her arms out of the T-shirt sleeves, then, her hands poking out from under the bottom, she snatched a blouse and pulled it back in with her.

Jack watched her, nonplussed. "How are you going to get there?"

She turned her back to him, wiggling around inside the T-shirt so that it looked like a sack full of animals with incompatible dispositions. "If you won't drive me, I'll find some other way. I'll walk."

She was going to do it, he realized through a fog of sheer incredulity. She *was* doing it. "What about room service?" Jack reminded her, thinking fast. "You want to lead him right to the trench? I mean, what if it *is* something your aunt's working on?"

"He won't be a problem." She whipped the T-shirt off her now clothed body and tossed it into the suitcase.

"Why not?"

"Because," she said calmly, snapping the suitcase shut, looking him in the eye, "we're going to take his distributor cap."

She didn't even blink.

NINE

The illuminated tunnel made by the Tracker's headlights disappeared momentarily as the truck lurched into and out of a particularly nasty rut. Then it shone in front of them again, lighting a narrow, leafy underpass through rain forest that was one good growth spurt away from swallowing the muddy road whole.

The Tracker side-slid into a wet, treacherous curve. Jack wrestled the truck into the switchback and fed the gas evenly, all the while swearing a blue streak. How Cathy had managed to drive on this road with her rented Jeep was a mystery he hadn't solved yet. But he'd shelved that question in favor of the more compelling one of why a road through the rain forest that by his calculations shouldn't have been used for two months was still there. He doubted that the local Taxticáns had been driving out to the ruins for Sunday picnics.

The truck fishtailed once more, and he swore again, then glanced toward Catherine and muttered, "*Lo siento.*"

Catherine braced herself against the door and gave him a quick glance over her shoulder. "No need to apologize," she said formally.

"I know that, *querida*. I apologize only when I feel like it."

She glanced at him again, frowning, and he grimaced. "I was making conversation, Cathy. There's been a distinct lack of it on this trip."

She cleared her throat. "I thought you'd want to concentrate on your driving," she said primly.

Jack grunted. "Driving this road after dark is something nobody *should* concentrate on."

She slid up straight in the seat, then folded her hands in her lap. "Well, then," she said finally, "what would you care to talk about?"

Jack muttered something under his breath and turned his attention back to the twin ruts winding through the jungle. He suspected that the lack of a topic for conversation was not what was keeping her silent.

More than suspected, he corrected himself. Knew for a fact. A woman who'd met "room service" at the door when he returned, dazzled him with a smile that could have heated up a dozen tortillas, and made some suggestive comment about how they'd want a big breakfast in the morning since they were sure to be hungry, had conversational skills she was holding back on.

Their intrepid tail had nearly stumbled over his feet imagining just what she was planning to do to work up such an appetite. He hadn't stood a chance, Jack reflected with grudging awe, especially not with the poor sucker's distributor cap stashed in her purse. Jack could almost feel sorry for him.

He would have, in fact, if he could have shared the stolen moment, so to speak, with his fellow perpetrator. But Cathy Moore wasn't sharing anything with anybody, least of all him.

With every passing kilometer since they'd left Taxticán she'd become more distant and less communicative—with the exception of a couple of pointed questions about her aunt.

He might have been able to tolerate the silence, he reflected, glancing toward Cathy's stiff, wary figure perched on the seat across from him, but the academic formality that had crept into her conversation was a little much to take considering the fires they'd lit in that hotel room. Her manner could have been lifted from a faculty tea party. Formal, strictly polite, and lukewarm.

Oh, he knew what she was doing. She didn't want to deal with the sparks they'd lit in that hotel room. There wasn't any way she could fit that particular scene into her career plan. And she was trying very hard to convince herself that she was going to complete her mission, restore her aunt's respectability, and go back to her research library, where any relationship she might have had with a wildcat computer hacker would be relegated to a minor footnote with a Latin abbreviation.

For some reason he couldn't justify and didn't intend to try, that galled him.

"This site," she said, clearing her throat, "where my aunt was digging—it was in connection with the codex, wasn't it?"

He gave her a quick look, then said, "Yeah."

"Did she find anything there?"

"Not that I know of."

"Nothing?"

"Nope."

"But how could she spend that much time and energy on a dig that wasn't yielding anything?"

"I don't know," Jack said. "You'd have to ask—"

"Ask my aunt," she finished. She propped her hand on the dashboard. "I hope to have the opportunity to do just that."

"I hope we both do, *querida*."

She set her lips together and cleared her throat one more time, then said with determined courtesy. "Well, at least we haven't gotten stuck yet."

As if perfectly timed for a bad joke, the Tracker sunk up to its bumper in the low-lying bog. Jack's blistering string of bilingual comments defied any apology he might have offered. He shouldered open the door, got out, and slammed it behind him hard enough to rock the truck.

"Do you need any help?" Catherine asked when he rolled down the back window and reached inside for the winch.

"Yeah, I do." He hefted the cable from the truck bed. "But I have a feeling you're not about to give me the kind I need."

Jack unwound the winch, propped the battery lantern in the driest of the ruts, and crouched down on his heels to attach the hook under the truck.

His passenger stayed where she was and said nothing. Whatever she was thinking, she wasn't giving him any clues.

He straightened and wound the free end of the cable around the base of the largest tree within reach, then took up the slack and started cranking.

Maybe if he asked her about the distributor cap in her purse she'd get real about what the hell they were doing out there, driving through the rain forest at midnight on a road that shouldn't still be there. Maybe she'd decide to turn around, drive back to Taxticán and pick up where they'd left off on that bed.

Yeah. And maybe during the ride back she'll figure out what exactly her aunt has to do with this particular trench on the site.

The truck inched out of the mud, and Jack undid the winch.

God, the way she'd asked him to kiss her, with that look in her eyes as much as with the whispered words . . . If she hadn't questioned him about the directions to this dig, they would have been doing more than whispering on that bed.

So maybe you shouldn't have told her anything. Just slipped in some vague line about computer codes and given her some other kind of distraction.

Swearing again, Jack climbed into the Tracker. He twisted the steering wheel sharply as the wheels spun, then found purchase.

Just who the hell did he think was distracting whom? Dammit, he'd seen Cathy's trusting, vulnerable gaze, heard that catch in her throat. If they took that last step he'd been hearing in her whispers, she'd expect things from him he wasn't prepared to give.

Honesty, for example.

So maybe you should have told her the whole truth.

He swore again.

He was nuts. That's all there was to it. He'd been driven over the edge by a sexy, Spanish-whispering, risqué-blouse-wearing con woman who was masquerading as a college professor.

So just get her to the so-called ruins, let her see for herself no one's been digging there for months, and take her back to Chetumal before she sets fire to any more of your plans, Gibraltar. Then make a phone call and do some ranting and raving about getting this operation wrapped up and over, and Cathy Moore out of your reach. Take up drinking, or whatever else you're going to have to do to push her out of your mind.

She leaned forward, peering out the front windshield, then glanced toward him. "I think it's just over this hill," she said tentatively, already reaching for the battery lantern between the two seats.

It was. The road topped the small rise and led into a clearing in front of the mound Catherine had taken for a Mayan ruin. Her Jeep was just where they'd left it a few hours ago, front wheels buried in the soft sides of the excavation trench, the vehicle resting on its axle in the mud at the edge of the ditch.

"Wait here a minute, all right?" he muttered, taking the lantern from her hand and sliding out of the Tracker. He slammed the door and strode toward the Jeep before she could get out and follow him.

To his relief, it didn't seem to have been disturbed. Her gear was still neatly packed behind the seat, nothing, apparently, missing. He let out a relieved breath. With any luck, they could be there and gone before whoever had been driving this road knew what they'd been up to.

He held the lantern toward the truck to

light Catherine's way, but, as he could have predicted, she hadn't waited for him to come back. She'd already walked over and was peering into the pitch-black trench as if she could see what was down there by sheer force of will.

She reached for the lantern. "Can I have that, please?"

Jack handed it over.

"Thank you," she said formally.

She was still talking as if they were guests in the faculty drawing room, he noted, but that didn't stop her from hiking up her split skirt and going down on hands and knees to shine the lantern into the trench. Her dark hair fell forward across her face and shadowed her light-colored shirt with the sleeves rolled up to the elbows. She was dressed like Madrid, was probably in her aunt's clothes. And the oversize shirt made her look sexier by disguising every detail of her torso.

Not that he needed any details, Jack reflected. His memory had been giving him muscle spasms in memorable places all the way from Taxticán.

She sat back on her heels after a moment, scanning the edge of the dig, which was already starting to be covered with the lush growth of the rain forest floor.

She hadn't found anything. She wouldn't either. Not on a dig that was intended primarily as a distraction for local looters.

The excavation extended sixty feet into the side of a small hill that could, with the right satellite scans, have been interpreted as a tomb or outbuilding to a main structure not yet unearthed. There had been no such satellite scans.

Sooner or later, he reflected, she'd realize that. He'd have to get her back to Chetumal before she did. And it would be sooner, if his guess was right. She had her hands in the dirt at the edge of the trench, sifting it through her fingers with the concentrated zeal he'd seen before in other good field archaeologists.

Cathy Moore wasn't headed back to a library. She'd caught the same kind of uncurable fever that drove her aunt, and she had all the right instincts to make it pay off. Even if she didn't know it yet.

"Have you got another light?" she asked him, setting the lantern down and getting to her feet.

"Yeah." He nodded. "In the truck."

"Good. I have a couple too—in the Jeep."

They could have provided their own light show by the time Cathy was satisfied she'd seen everything there was to see in the trench, Jack decided. Leaning against her canted Jeep, swatting mosquitoes, he'd waited patiently for her to finish her explorations, even to the point of matching her excessively polite dealings with his own whenever she'd requested his assistance.

But when she finally put the flashlights back into the Jeep, leaned over the seat, and pulled out the heavy canvas tent, Jack's patience reached its limit. He took the bulky sack from her arms, dropped it into the front seat, and slammed the door on it.

"What," he said, echoing her rigid courtesy, "are you planning to do with that?"

She blinked at him. "Set it up."

"What for?"

"We're staying here. I can't really see anything until daylight."

He was shaking his head before she finished the sentence. "No," he said emphatically.

She didn't respond well to the pronouncement. "All right," she told him calmly, "*I'm* staying here, then. You can go back if you like."

"I do like. And so do you, *querida*. I'm not

staying. You're not staying. Nobody's staying."

"Why not?"

"It's illegal, for one thing!"

"Illegal?" Her eyebrows rose. "When did illegality ever stop you before?"

"When did it ever stop *me*?" Outraged at the unfairness of turning his own argument against him, Jack slapped his hand against the window of the Jeep. This was what he got for being partially truthful, he decided, meeting Catherine's irate gaze with his own. He got accused of illegality. By a woman with a stolen distributor cap in her purse.

"As a matter of fact," she went on, crossing her dirty hands over her chest, "when did anything ever stop you from doing exactly what you wanted to do?"

"What are you talking about?" He slapped the Jeep again. It settled a little lower into the trench, and he stepped back, scowling at it.

Catherine looked at it in mild alarm, but apparently she wasn't going to let concern for either her Jeep or Jack set her off her purpose. "You," she said accusingly. "You have no compunctions about anything that you do. I don't see why a marginally illegal—"

"No *compunctions*?"

She stopped talking.

"No compunctions," he repeated, ready to defend himself yet irritatingly, uncharacteristically, at a loss for words. She did that to him, he decided. Probably on purpose. "What the hell is a compunction anyway?"

"It's an ethical standard that prevents a civilized person from just indulging in whatever he—"

"*Indulging?* You're accusing me of indulging?" He hadn't done anything close to indulging since she'd banged on his door and demanded his computer files. Well, maybe one thing, he admitted. Close anyway.

"Yes," she shot back. "You just indulge your impulses in every—"

"Wait a minute," Jack said, his mouth curving with a slight dawning-of-recognition smile. "This is about what happened at the hotel, isn't it?"

"I don't know—"

"In Taxticán. Two hours ago. In the room. On the bed. That's what this is about, isn't it?"

Her mouth worked as she stared a hole into his forehead. She wanted, in the worst way, to contradict him, he guessed. But she just wasn't dishonest enough to do it. "You just . . . do or say whatever you want, don't you?"

He leaned back against the Jeep, his own arms crossed like hers. "And you didn't want it?" Jack asked softly into the humming darkness.

"I wanted information!"

"Information."

"Yes! About my aunt!"

Maybe she *was* dishonest enough, Jack decided grimly. Maybe that was part of her newly discovered slate of instincts.

If it was, she was carrying it just one step too far. There was a time and a place for the truth, after all.

And she was a woman who brought out that particular impulse in Jack Gibraltar. It didn't have much to do with self-protection. The part of his brain that did made a brief, feeble protest but attracted very little of his attention. *That* had gone down for the count in Taxticán.

They stared at each other while the chattering night life of the tropical forest filled in the silence, punctuated by another howler monkey call.

Her eyes flicked toward it.

"Monkey," he said automatically.

"Oh. Well, then."

Well, then. "That's a piece of information about the rain forest," Jack offered. "They sound just like jaguars. This is a place where it's hard to tell the benign species from the predators."

"I've noticed that, Mr. Gibraltar."

Mr. Gibraltar. Mouth quirked, Jack pulled open the Jeep's door and yanked out the tent.

It must have been one of Madrid's prizes, he decided as he dropped the sack on the ground and loosened the draw cord. The tent measured twelve by twelve, with an awning off the front that doubled the space. Since fortunately the night was warm, Jack decided to set up just the frame and canvas roof and cover the whole thing with mosquito netting.

"This is from Madrid's closet?" he grunted.

"Why, yes," she said.

"I thought so. She's a firm believer in British Colonial style when it comes to camping out."

"I suppose she is."

Jack gave her a short, pointed look as he pulled out yards of mosquito netting. "Don't expect it from me. I don't drink tea and I left my pith helmet at home." He grinned at her. "And I sleep in the nude."

"I wouldn't expect anything else, Mr. Gibraltar," she told him, her jaw clenched.

He would have had the tent up in less than fifteen minutes if it weren't for Catherine's courteous offers of help and determinedly polite rejoinders to his goading replies.

There was a double-size foam mattress stashed behind the seat in the Jeep, as well as a lace-shaded battery lamp Madrid must have found in some Victorian-replica gift shop for the colonially displaced. Jack got them both out and set them under the netting, then unrolled the mattress.

"You planning to share this, Professor?" he asked her, careful to sound tactful.

"I beg your pardon?"

"I don't have a mattress," he explained. "Of course, I could sleep on the ground."

"You could . . ." For an instant something flashed in her gaze that Jack found unreasonably satisfying, but she got it under control before she spoke. "No, I'm sure that's not necessary. You must have your own sleeping bag, and under the circumstances, we can certainly share a mattress."

"You want to say that in Spanish, *querida*? It sounds better."

"I'm afraid I've used up all my Spanish

vocabulary, Mr. Gibraltar," she told him sweetly. "What they teach at college goes only so far, you know."

"I figured you hadn't learned it on the streets."

To his disgust, she didn't quite rise to the bait. She opened her mouth to snap at him, then closed it, dusted off her hands on her equally dusty skirt, and gave him a calm, St.-Catherine-with-a-Ph.D. smile. "I learned enough to say, 'No, thank you,' Mr. Gibraltar. That should suffice in the future."

Oh, it should? He was that resistible, was he? To the woman who'd been whispering Spanish suggestions in his ear a few hours ago?

"Fine," he said shortly.

She nodded, steepled her fingers, nodded, then snapped, "Fine," like a dropped gauntlet.

"Why don't you drop the college-professor act?"

"I beg your pardon?"

"As of now, I'd suggest, Cathy," he said softly.

She blinked. "Well, really, Jack, it's hardly an act. I *am* a college professor. To pretend otherwise would be—"

"Don't say it," he gritted out.

She blinked again. "I beg your pardon?"

"Because if you do," he threatened, "I'm not going to be responsible for what happens next."

"What?"

"With my bare hands. On that mattress you think we're going to share without anything *untenable* happening on it."

Her mouth tightened, but something definitely loosened in her narrowed gaze. Definitely, Jack noted in triumph.

"Do you think you could *ever* make a point without being crude?" she snapped at him.

"No. Because you wouldn't get it unless it threw you down on the bed and ripped off your clothes."

"Maybe if you state it in a more civilized way, I'd have a better chance!"

"You want civilized, Professor, stick to the library. You want action, on the other hand," he added, a corner of his mouth hitching up in a smug grin, "you can come to me."

She shoved her thumbs into the waistband of her skirt as if she didn't trust herself not to make the first move toward violence. "I most definitely do *not* want action, Mr. Gibraltar, and if I did, I wouldn't want it from you!"

"Oh, no?" He took a small step closer to her. "And here I thought you just couldn't keep your hands off my hard disk."

Outrage charged the air around her. She pulled her hands out of her skirt and crossed her arms in front of her, glaring at him. "You are utterly," she said, enunciating each word, "irredeemably, reprehensibly, academically—"

"What?" he challenged her.

She was seething, so angry she gave off heat he could feel. For several charged moments she kept her mouth clamped shut and her arms tightly crossed over her chest.

Then she said it. "*Untenable.*"

The rest of Jack's mouth curved into a smile. "I thought so," he said softly. He closed the last of the distance between them, pulled her toward him by the shoulders, and brought his mouth down onto hers.

TEN

Catherine was too startled to make any protest beyond a soft murmur deep in her throat that Jack ignored completely. He threaded his fingers into her hair and tipped her head up to his, holding her flush against his body, with his strong arms around her back.

For the span of a few resolution-crumbling thoughts she pressed her hands against his shoulders, pushing him away, but he touched her mouth with the barest pressure, moving his lips lightly and sensually and with exquisite sensitivity until she made another soft sound and opened her mouth against his.

Jack's hands tightened on the back of her head, and his kiss deepened with sudden urgent pressure. He filled her mouth with the hot, demanding penetration of his tongue, claiming her with a searing kiss of such heat and passion, all the nerve endings from her toes to her hair roots curled and stretched. She responded instinctively—to the way he held her, the taste of his mouth, the sensuality of his tongue moving over hers. Her throat-deep moan was a sound of abandoned sensuality.

"No, Cathy?" he whispered against her mouth in a question that made no sense to her. "You don't want this?"

Her eyes opened slowly; awareness of the words was still to come into her passionate gaze. "What?" she murmured, dazed.

"This," he said, bending to her again. "Me. Kissing you. Holding you." He trailed his mouth along the line of her jaw to her ear. "Laying you across that mattress and running my hands up under your shirt. Touching you. With my hands, with my mouth. Do you want that, *querida*? Do you want me to do that, Cathy?"

His hair was limned with gold from the lantern behind him, but in the shadows his eyes were a midnight blue and they held an intensity that made her knees go weak. She realized with a shiver of emotion that stopped her heart that his hands were trembling.

He wanted her. He wanted her so much

he was trembling. He was asking her to take him.

Around them, the noisy chatter of bird life in the rain forest filtered through the thick growth of plants, muted by moist, scented air and underscored by the hum of insects. Above them, the tangled foliage of the tropical forest stirred with a breeze that seemed to echo her own husky, whispered reply. It was no language of words.

"Say it, Cathy," Jack urged her. "Tell me."

His lips brushed against her skin, and his breath on her cheek stirred sensations as lush as the wakening of the jungle after a rain. She felt them now, pouring through her, pulsing with primal female power.

She threaded her own hands into his gold-tipped hair, clasping him with insistence and demand that equaled his to her. "Touch me," she demanded. "I want you to. I want you to touch me. Do it."

His eyes locked on hers, he slid his hands down her back to the waistband of her skirt, slipped his fingers inside, then slowly, carefully, pulled her blouse out of her skirt. The erotic feel of the soft cotton skimming over her sent a shiver scrambling up her spine. When his warm, strong hands slipped into the back of her skirt and pressed against her skin, she made a sound of pleasure, clinging to Jack's shoulders for support as her bones seemingly melted.

Her eyes closed, then opened, and she met Jack's burning blue eyes. She knew her own languid gaze made no attempt to hide the heady sensations that raced through her.

"You make me feel like the rain forest," she murmured, past caring whether she could be understood. The fire inside her demanded that she commit herself to it with no reserve, no explanations, no footnotes. "You make me feel wild," she told him, her head thrown back, her eyes half closed. "Alive. Humming with life. Singing."

"Ah . . . Cathy." Her name came out on a husky groan. The sound of it thrilled her. "*Canta conmigo ahora, querida.*"

She wanted to. She wanted to sing with him. More than she'd ever wanted anything in her life.

Jack.

The sudden focusing of intent in his expression made her realize she must have said his name aloud. His square jaw was clenched with the effort of control. The mobile mouth was still, with no trace of either irony or exit lines, and the blue eyes blazed with primitive plans she couldn't mistake. Pressed against him, wrapped in his arms, she felt surrounded by him the way the forest surrounded their small clearing.

Beneath her hands his shoulders flexed as he slid his hands down to cup her buttocks and pull her more securely against him.

Through the confining zipper of his jeans Catherine could feel him against her, hard, hot, undeniably aroused. The honesty of Jack's need spoke to her as eloquently as the murmured Spanish love words, and she responded to it with a small cry and a sinuous movement of her hips that fitted him into the niche of her thighs.

With one strong movement he lifted her, parting her thighs and holding her intimately against the ridge of flesh that defined his urgent desire.

He thrust against her once, hard, with force that made her breath catch, then his strong fingers kneaded her buttocks, smoothing and shaping the resilient flesh. "That's what I want, *querida*," he said, his voice raw. "That's the way I want you. That's how much."

She watched his mouth as he said the words, and deep inside her, dormant yearnings wakened to life. "Sí," she whispered fiercely. "That way. *Hazlo exactamente así. Ahora.* I want—"

With a muffled groan he cut off her words with a fierce kiss. It was demanding, rough, and hard, and it was exactly what she wanted from him.

Needing to touch him, Catherine flattened her palms against him, then moved her hands lower and fumbled with the button of his jeans.

Jack let her slide down his legs until she stood on the soft ground, then, still kissing her, he brought his hands around to the front of her waistband and released the first button of her skirt. The back of his knuckles caressing her stomach through the silk of her panties sent waves of shivery pleasure through her, making her fingers clumsy. But the urge to touch him, to feel the velvet hardness that pulsed just beneath her fingers, drove her. She managed to free the button and pull down the zipper.

Jack's hands went still, and his mouth separated from hers by the space of a breath as she slipped her hand inside his pants.

He was taut, hard, like warm, smooth obsidian, and when she sheathed him in her hand he shuddered and made a sound deep in his throat, and his hands gripped her waist convulsively. His fingers dug into the soft flesh around her hips, and Catherine reveled in his reaction to her. She felt unfurled, life-filled, flushed with feminine power, as earthy and rich as the rain forest itself, and she loved it.

When Jack covered her hand and tried to tug it away from him, she resisted.

"No more, *querida*," he rasped. "Not unless you want it standing up against the Jeep."

She wanted it any way she could have it. Every way she could have it. Again and again, until she couldn't stand up anymore.

"Yes," she hissed.

"Yes," Jack repeated, claiming her mouth again.

She expected him to do just what he'd suggested, but instead he scooped her up and carried her into the tent.

He dropped to his knees beside the mattress and settled her on her back, then sat on his heels.

Instinctively, she reached for him again. "Jack . . . don't you want—"

"Yeah, babe," he said, his voice raw. "I want you like hell on fire." His mouth curved in a slow smile. "How about you?" he asked her.

She knew what he was asking: for an unfeigned response, and she could no more have denied him than she could have denied herself. Deliberately, she raised herself on her elbows, then, her eyes locked on his, released the top button of her blouse.

She caught the blaze in his eyes as she moved her hand to the next button and unfastened it. His deliberate, direct appraisal of her body made her feel sexy, abandoned, shamelessly seductive. The kind of woman who went trekking off into the jungle in search of lost ruins. The kind of woman who left cryptic notes on her refrigerator and expected to be followed. The kind of woman who *was* followed—to Mexico, to the jungle, into a tent draped with mosquito netting and lit by the golden glow of an outside lantern.

He let her unbutton the blouse all the way, touching her only with his dark gaze. She leaned back on both elbows, letting the blouse fall open to reveal her breasts.

Jack leaned toward her, slid onto the mattress, and as he had in the hotel room in Taxticán, brought his mouth down to the rigid peak of her breast and touched it with his tongue.

Catherine gave a sharp gasp, straining

toward him, arching her back to bring her breast closer to the sweet torment his mouth could give her. Jack's hands slid around her arched back, supporting her, then, slowly, with exquisite care, he drew the crest of her breast into his mouth—first one, and then the other, caressing and shaping her with his hot velvet tongue and sensual, seeking lips.

Wave after wave of sensation washed over her, filling her with pleasure so sharp, an incoherent, yearning cry tore from her own throat. She reached for him blindly, her hands on his hips inside the loosened jeans, his name a ragged demand in her voice.

Jack's control nearly shattered. He'd wanted Cathy since he'd caught sight of her in La Stela, and he'd wanted her like this—wild, abandoned, passionate, with no pretense and nothing held back.

His hunger to be inside her was so primal he was mindless with it, but even beyond that was his need to drive her over the edge with him, to make her want him every way a woman who knows her own mind can want a man. And he wanted to hear her say it. In English, in Spanish, in the language of the jungle night around them. Cathy's soul-deep desire was like nothing he'd ever wanted from a woman before, and nothing he could live without since he'd heard it.

Still kissing her, he shoved his jeans down so that he could pull his legs out of them, then, with the same rough urgency, he unfastened the buttons of her skirt and yanked it off from under her hips.

When he slid his hand up the inside of her thigh she cried out and opened herself to him. The urge to take the invitation, to take her hard and fast and immediately, was a white-hot impulse burning through him, but he held it back.

He slid up along her body, threaded his hand into the silky hair at the nape of her neck, and kissed her again, letting her feel the savagery of his desire in the rough pressure of his mouth on hers.

She circled his neck with one hand and kissed him back, and when he stroked higher on her thigh, where the dark triangle of soft, curling hair marked the center of her femininity, she made a sound that tasted of something so sweet.

"So you want me to touch you, Cathy?" he murmured against her lips. "Like this?"

"Yes. Touch me."

"Tell me what it feels like. Tell me what you want."

Her nails raked down his chest to his stomach, then her warm, soft palm enclosed him.

"I want you inside me, Jack. Now. *Ahora. Satisfaceme.Te deseo. Por favor,* Jack."

The urgent throb of his need was no longer controllable. He slid his hand under her knee, lifting her and opening her to his slow, deep entry. When he was sheathed inside her, holding her, murmuring love words that came without thought, feeling her deep, intense shudders of pleasure, he started to move in slow, piercing, deliberate consummation that spoke ancient messages of men and women.

She was part of him. She was a part of him he'd lost and hadn't realized he could find. The sounds she made when he drew back and then moved inside her again vibrated somewhere deep in his own body and his own soul. *Oh, babe, you're mine now. You belong to me.*

Moving with her, watching her face, he was aware that her mouth had curved in a slow, sensual smile. "Is that the truth?" she said.

He smiled back at her. "Yeah, babe. That's the truth."

"And here I was thinking that you belonged to me."

His smile faded as she wrapped her legs around his hips and a shudder of pleasure exploded through him. "Yes, Cathy," he murmured, his voice husky. "That's the truth too. That's the absolute . . . irrefutable . . . irredeemable . . ." He kissed her fiercely, hungrily, without control. He held her, running his hands over her body, smoothing his palms along her thighs, losing himself in sheer mindless sensation.

He thrust deeply into her again and again, making both of them cry out with shared pleasure and urgency and unbearable need that exploded into shimmering, singing ecstasy. It pulsed through him like the life of the jungle and was given voice in Cathy's sweet, wordless cry of completion.

For a long time Jack didn't let her go, rolling to his side, cradling her head on his shoulder, stroking her back, murmuring her name while the battery-powered lantern outside the tent grew dimmer, then finally went out completely.

"Cathy?" he murmured softly.

She made some sound, but it wasn't an answer, and Jack realized she must be asleep.

In his arms. On her mattress. In her aunt's tent. In the Taxticán jungle.

He wasn't sure what that meant.

And he'd never particularly liked uncertainty. It ought to make him nervous, he reflected.

Hell, it did make him nervous. It scared the pants off him.

He glanced down at his pantless body, still entwined with Cathy's skirtless body. The sight was a definite distraction. It was a magnificently, beautifully, satisfyingly skirtless body. He wrapped his hand around her leg to pull her closer. She felt incredibly good, even asleep, silent, trusting, vulnerable, her mouth soft and her fingers curled into his chest. There was nothing wild about her but the memory of it.

But it was a hell of a memory, Jack acknowledged, feeling a reaction in that distinctly male part of him.

"Cathy," he murmured softly, "we have to talk about this." He stopped himself, frowning. "No. No, that's not what I meant. I meant . . ." He stroked her hair, listening to the hum of the tropical forest outside the mosquito netting. "This wasn't part of the song, *mi amor*. I was thinking, you know, something along the lines of humming in the shower. I didn't know it was going to be an opera." *And a damn good opera, at that.* A *fine* opera. With a magnificent heroine—passionate, ardent, strong. Sexy as hell.

"Maybe it's not in the script, but I want to sing with you again," he murmured to her. "A lot of times."

She was asleep, he reminded himself. He was talking to a woman who was asleep. Telling her things he'd never intended to say.

He wasn't sure what the hell had happened here, but something had. Something that didn't have a damn thing to do with Madrid, or the codex, or Blasquo. Something significant. Catastrophic, maybe.

And that was the truth.

The sun had climbed high enough to make the tropical forest steam when Jack roused himself out of a short night's sleep and glanced around him to get his bearings.

The Taxticán jungle hadn't changed. Madrid's tent was still pitched at the edge of the excavation trench. The earth hadn't moved since the last time they'd made love on it. There was something definitely wrong with this picture though. He knew it even before he was awake.

Jack sat up, snagged a handful of the mosquito netting, and lifted it. The woman who was supposed to be in his arms was crouched over the far end of the trench—half in it, really—digging in the soft, muddy earth with God knows what she'd found for an excavation tool. Her fingernails, probably, if she hadn't located anything more appropriate.

Cathy Moore, with her uncanny instincts and tenacious persistence and inconveniently analytical mind, was digging for evidence in a trench that just might, for all he knew, turn some up.

He muttered an oath, dropped the netting, and added a few more words for good measure while pulling his jeans from the ground cloth. He yanked them on, then shoved a hand through his hair, dragged his fingers down his stubbled chin, and stepped outside.

She glanced up when he walked toward her. He recognized the look. Dirt on her hands, an oh-what-a-beautiful-morning smile on her face, the excitement of archaeological discovery in her eyes.

He was about to erase that excitement, he realized suddenly.

"Look at this, Jack."

He stopped moving, his gaze fixed on her tangled, shiny, uncombed hair. It smelled like flowers. He wasn't close enough to smell it, but he didn't need to be. He'd spent the night smelling it, feeling it. And it felt like silk.

He felt like dragging her back into her aunt's tent and reacquainting both of them with the finer details of the night's occupation, but he had a hunch that she would differ with his purpose.

"You're not *looking,*" she said.

"Yes, I am."

"At the *trench*, Jack."

"The trench."

She got to her feet, dusted off her hands, then turned toward him, reaching out to touch his arm. She pulled back just at the last moment, but then, a little tentatively, went ahead and touched him. He felt it all the way down to his bare feet.

"Jack . . ." she said softly. Her voice had the same husky note he'd heard in it the night before. "I never said how much it means to me that you told me about this . . . the message."

He shut his eyes for a moment. His hand found her waist and slipped around it, caressing the gentle, sweet curve just above her hip while possible responses came into his mind.

"Look," she said, her voice confidential, trusting. "See this fern? Where it's been uprooted? It's still *green*."

Jack shifted his gaze to what she held in her hands. A fern, a little wilted, but still, as she'd said, green.

"It's just been dug," she told him. "There's been recent digging all along this trench, every five feet. Systematic. According to a plan."

Jack's eyes traveled down to the trench, back along the length of it to the Jeep, back again to Cathy's uprooted fern.

It had just been dug, all right. Recently. As in yesterday. "Son of a bitch," he said softly but with feeling.

She misinterpreted the feeling. Her hand tightened on his arm, sending a vibrant, ardent message he couldn't afford to hear.

"This is an active dig, Jack! Someone's working it!" Excitement vibrated in her voice. She swept a strand of hair out of her face, leaving another streak of dirt across her cheekbone, like a punctuation mark to her pleased, excited expression.

"Someone's working it, all right, Cath," he agreed, his voice grim. "The question is who."

"What do you mean, *who*? It's my aunt's dig. She discovered it. She's the one who's disappeared into the jungle for—"

"Was," he said succinctly, peering down at the trench again.

"What?"

"*Was* your aunt's dig, Cathy."

Some of the light went out in her face. She took a step back from him, away from his encircling arm, and turned toward the trench, her arms crossing in front of her, hugging her elbows.

He reluctantly hooked his thumbs into his jeans pockets. "Look at this," he told her, and then waited until she had. "It's systematic, all right. Like someone didn't see any scans or get any lab results."

She peered along the trench, frowning, then finally looked up at him. She was resisting the obvious conclusion, and he knew it.

He said it for her. "Someone's fishing here, Cath. Someone who didn't dig this trench in the first place."

Her face clouded. "You mean—"

"Looters."

A corner of her mouth tightened briefly, as if she had to work at keeping her face neutral, but the wash of swift disappointment in her eyes pulled at him, stabbing him with guilt for taking away her near discovery.

He dismissed the guilt, threading his fingers through his hair and then shoving his hand back into his pocket.

What was he, nuts? What was he feeling guilty for? Every word he was saying was the truth, for God's sake. They had to get out of there.

"You know how fast looters move in on an abandoned dig."

"I know it can be an occasional problem," she said, "but I don't—"

He swore again, roughly enough to cut off the careful academic assessment of the *occasional problem*. "Get real, Cath. They're armed, they're dangerous, and they're everywhere. And they'll be back. We may have had problems dealing with Blasquo and his cronies, but this is another step up in the trouble department. It looks like they're working every day." He let out a breath. "And we're going to be gone when they get here."

"But we just arrived."

A lot of assurance had leaked out of her statement by the time she got to the last word. It wasn't hard to read the tone of voice. The vibrant, spirited woman who'd dueled with him in Chetumal and the room in Taxticán, who'd matched him word for word, sigh for sigh, touch for touch in the night just past, was beginning to give in to some old self-doubts. About her assumptions, about the outcome of this maneuver. He felt his chest constrict, as if there weren't quite enough oxygen in the steamy clearing.

He knew what was going to happen. She was going to look up at him, and he was going to read something he didn't want to see in her eyes: questions about whether her recent choice of a leading man had been a good idea. About the wisdom of this particular quest. About whether she should have been there in the first place.

And for some reason he didn't have time to go into at the moment, that was going to hurt.

"Cathy . . . listen, when we get back you can make inquiries. About the dig. Your aunt. Whatever."

Her honest, probing gaze caught his. "When we get back where?" she asked. "Back here?"

He closed his eyes again, getting a grip on this situation. "First things first, okay? We get out of here, then we talk."

"About what?" she said. Her voice was steady, but he could see the doubt creeping into her eyes.

"About last night, Cath."

For a moment he saw something in her face that tightened the band around his lungs another notch. Something that indicated she'd been deeply wounded.

He silently cursed himself for saying the wrong thing at the wrong time, with all the right intentions.

"Cathy, what I meant was—"

"There's no need to explain," she said quickly. "In fact, I don't think it would be a good idea at all. As a matter of fact, I think I'd rather you didn't explain." She didn't call him *Mr. Gibraltar*, but she came close to it. Jack narrowed his eyes, frowning. "So," she said, "first things first, right? We'll have to get the Jeep out of the trench, and get it running."

"Yeah."

"Yes. Of course. Maybe the gas line problem isn't . . ."

She hesitated just long enough for him to wonder if she was going to say *untenable*.

" . . . a serious problem," she finished.

"Yeah."

"Well." She gave him the kind of smile he didn't want to see along with an expression he couldn't interpret. "I suppose we should get started."

Jack didn't like that she'd gone polite on him again. He didn't like it at all.

"I assume you have a plan, right?" she asked him crisply.

Now she thought he didn't have a plan? He nodded once and pinned her with an insulted man-who's-been-underestimated look.

He had a plan.

He was going to get both the Jeep and Catherine out of there. Then he was going to take her back to Chetumal and make love to her until her toes curled and she couldn't remember to ask questions he didn't know how to answer or give him expressions he didn't want to interpret.

Then he was going to start all over and do it again.

"All right," he said with just as much determination as she had. "Let's do it."

ELEVEN

By the time the Jeep rolled into the muddy lot in front of the cantina, Catherine was too sore to step foot out of the Jeep, too hungry to worry about the stolen distributor cap she still had in her purse, and too tired to keep wondering just what Jack had meant when he'd said they had things to talk about.

What things?

He got out of the Tracker, unhooked the Jeep, and rewound the winch, moving with the brisk efficiency of practice. Catherine watched, quelling a twinge of resentment that was based on something far too deep to consider.

At least until she got some answers.

They hadn't talked while he winched her stuck Jeep out of the trench and maneuvered it onto the road. And she hadn't pushed the point after he'd given her that guilty look, blue eyes regretful and blond hair falling in his face and his jeans dragged down over his hips by his hands in his pockets.

That look had stirred something deep inside her that had scared her. How dare he look guilty after what they'd done the night before? It made her think he had something to hide. It made her think she shouldn't have . . .

It made her *think*, dammit, when that was the last thing she wanted to do. If she started thinking, she had a horrible, desperate feeling she'd start remembering. What she'd said. What they'd done.

What she'd felt.

Her throat tightened, and she was suddenly too aware of the heavy thud of her heart.

She felt as if they were partners. Soulmates. Lovers. He'd trusted her with the truth about his computer network message, and she'd trusted him with . . . everything.

No, she told herself. Not everything. She couldn't have trusted him with everything.

Because if she had, the logical conclusion was that she was already involved in something she was going to very much regret.

And she couldn't afford to regret it.

Catherine closed her eyes and rested her forehead on the steering wheel. She couldn't even afford to think about regretting it. Because that would mean that something she'd entered into with her whole soul, her whole heart, *everything*, had been a mistake.

The smell of hot coffee drifted in through the open window of the Jeep, strong enough to make her lift her head and pry her cramped fingers off the steering wheel.

Jack was standing beside the Jeep, carrying two mugs and offering one to her.

It smelled too good to pass up, she decided.

He smiled at her when she reached for the mug, his wide, mobile mouth turning up in that sexy smile that insinuated more than it should have. Her heart did a frantic dance for a few moments before it resumed its steady beat.

"Breakfast?" he asked her.

She nodded, shouldered the Jeep door open, and followed Jack into the cantina's small dining room.

Their meal of tortillas, beans, and mashed bananas was brought by a silent waitress who quickly left them to tend to another table, where a couple was chatting in a Mayan dialect Catherine didn't understand. Jack left her to go off in search of coffee and information, and came back with a stoneware pitcher.

"Blasquo's crony is still here, Cath," he said, refilling their mugs. "Word is that he wasn't very happy this morning, when his car wouldn't start."

"Oh."

"Yeah."

"Did he . . . check under the hood?"

"If he didn't, I'm sure someone else did."

"Oh."

He said more softly, "Don't start feeling guilty about it, *querida*. You did what you had to do."

"I wasn't feeling—" She bit the word off. It wasn't a word she wanted to raise between them. Besides, she *had* been feeling it.

"Jack . . ."

"No word about your aunt. No one around here has seen her."

"But they wouldn't, would they?"

"What do you mean?"

"She'd be underground. She wouldn't let anyone know she was here."

He put down his fork. "There's no way anyone could be working that dig and not have the locals know about it. Anyone working that dig would need supplies, workers, gas for the trucks. Believe me, Madrid's not here."

"Madrid's not—"

He picked up his fork again. "Right."

Instinct told her to watch him a little more closely. He looked ready to start rubbing the back of his neck.

"Jack," she said.

"What?"

"Look at me while you say that. *Por favor.*"

"Say what?"

"Madrid's not here."

He shook his head, leaned back in his chair as if he couldn't believe he was being asked to do such a thing.

And he didn't do it, she noticed.

"Cath," he told her instead, "our best bet is to go back to Chetumal, ask some questions. Who knows, maybe Madrid has left a message on her machine or something. We can check out the locals, then maybe do some research at the university." He gave her a faint smile. "We'll leave right after breakfast, how's that?"

She stared at him, while dangerous emotions knifed through her. She pushed them away. She had a job to do. A reason to be here besides Jack. A mission to fulfill. "No," she said.

"What do you mean no?"

"I mean it, Jack," she said. "Go ahead if you want to. I'm staying."

He put his fork down again. "No, you're not. You're leaving. With me. Today."

"Why should I?"

"Because your aunt's not here. Because Blasquo's henchman is. Because the site is being looted, for God's sake!"

"My aunt might need help."

"She doesn't, dammit!"

"How do I know that?"

"Because I'm telling you."

Catherine stared at him, silent, her mouth set.

"Cath," he said, his voice low and persuasive, his damned blue eyes pleading and seductive, "can't you trust me on this? Just this time?"

She swallowed hard. "Why should I?"

"You did last night."

"Yes," she said. "I did. And look where it got me."

He flinched. Not much, but enough to tell her she'd hit home. His mouth tightened, and anger flared in the beautiful blue eyes.

"It got you right where you belonged,

querida," he said. "Where did you think you were headed at the end of this mission? Back to the library? You think that's where you belong? You think that's the real you?"

"Maybe it is! How do you know what the real me is?"

"Well, if that's what you wanted, why didn't you stay there in the first place?"

"I wanted to find out what happened to my aunt!"

"Why?"

She didn't answer him.

"So *she* can go back to the library with a squeaky-clean reputation and all her academic respectability restored? You think Madrid really cares about that?"

"*I* care!"

"Why?"

"Because!"

"Because *why*, dammit!"

"So I can know she's not a crook!" Catherine blurted out.

Stunned silence stretched across the small table. The waitress was standing in the kitchen doorway, her eyebrows raised into question marks. The other patrons were looking away, careful not to move or intrude.

Jack let out a long breath, regarding her

with dawning insight and something that could have been read as empathy. As understanding.

Her throat tightened. She was dangerously close to some emotion she didn't want to feel. She didn't dare feel that level of vulnerability. She was already vulnerable enough. Too vulnerable.

"Your aunt's not a crook, Cathy."

Her eyes widened. "What?"

"The codex—it's the real thing. Authentic."

"*What?*"

He dragged his hand down his face, looking up at her. "Blasquo ran a scam on us all. By declaring the codex a fake, he's free to sell it on the black market and make a fortune on it. If it's real, it has to stay in the country of origin."

She wrapped her hands around her coffee cup, clutching it as she tried to sort out the story. "But why didn't you just deny his story and announce that it was authentic?"

"We didn't have enough evidence. And he had the codex."

It was beginning to make sense. "So you surprised Blasquo," she said slowly, "by corroborating his announcement."

"Yeah. Madrid figured that would keep him

from selling to any kind of black-market buyer until *he* could provide evidence of authenticity. It would slow him down a couple weeks anyway. Enough time for your aunt to do some more investigating."

Catherine's stomach churned into a knot, tightening around the bitter realization that she should have figured this out sooner. That it should have made sense a lot sooner. "And that's what she's doing, isn't it? She's looking for more evidence."

He nodded, wary.

Her mouth hardened. "Then there's no way I'm leaving."

A flicker of dismay crossed his face, then regret. "Yes, you are."

"Tell me *one thing* that will make me leave."

He fiddled with his coffee cup. "You're in the wrong place, Cath. Your aunt's not here. She's in Guatemala."

Catherine's hands balled into fists with enough force to make her fingernails dig into her palms, but she was unaware of the pain. "How do you know that?" she asked, her throat tense.

"I've been in touch with her."

"In touch with her."

"Cathy . . ."

"And what are you doing here with me?"

"Trying to keep you out of—"

"Out of the way?"

He closed his eyes. When he opened them, they were bleak. And guilty. "Tell me to go to hell if you want, Cath. Tell me to—"

"And all this talk about where I *belong*? In my aunt's tent? With you?"

"That doesn't have anything to do with this."

It took her a moment to understand what he'd said. His voice was fading in and out oddly. "Oh, I think it does. I think you were keeping me just where I *belong, querido*. Out of the way."

"Cath, don't do this."

But what else was she going to do? She swallowed hard and lifted her chin. "I'll tell you something, Jack," she said softly. "It was one hell of a good con."

Jack watched her push back the chair and walk across the room, her back straight, her head high. Then he propped his elbows on the table and covered his face with his hands, his teeth gritted together to keep himself from saying anything else to her.

He'd already sunk himself in a deep enough

hole. He turned around when he heard the door to the cantina close behind her and half rose from his chair to go after her, then sat back down again. He didn't doubt she had every intention of locking him out of their room. He might as well just wait her out.

He lasted five minutes before the urge to pace got him out of the chair. He stalked into the cantina's small office and headed for the phone.

"*Por favor?*" he muttered at the sleepy-eyed boy behind the desk.

"*Sí.*"

The connection was bad.

"Jack!" Madrid boomed over the line. "Where have you been? I've been trying to call you for a couple of days. We've got all the evidence we need."

"Good," he muttered dispiritedly.

"Now you don't have to keep Blasquo off my back."

"Yeah."

"Is something wrong, Jack? You sound strange."

"I'm fine."

"It's not Catherine, is it?" Madrid's voice turned worried. "She's not mixed up with Blasquo, is she?"

Jack waited a moment, his jaw clenched, before he answered. "No, Madrid. She's out of Blasquo's hands. And I don't think she has any interest in what he's up to anymore."

"Oh, good."

"Yeah," Jack echoed ironically. "Good."

"I do appreciate your keeping her out of trouble. You've done a very good job of it."

A very good job. The unintended echo of Cathy's bitter accusation hit him like a fist in the stomach.

"Yeah," he said finally before he slammed the phone down and let out a string of Spanish curses that left the sleepy desk clerk blinking at him in awe.

It took him another fifteen minutes to decide he wasn't capable of waiting Catherine out. Lock or no lock, tears or fangs, he was going to talk to her, dammit.

It took him exactly two minutes longer to discover she wasn't in the room.

She'd left on the road back toward Chetumal, the cantina's owner told him.

With all her luggage.

In his truck.

TWELVE

"*De nada*," Jack said as the man he'd stopped for climbed into the rattletrap pickup and pulled the door shut behind him. He'd made a practice of offering rides since he'd left Taxticán. Because the pickup's top speed seemed to be twenty miles an hour, stopping for a passenger didn't slow him down much, and he had an acute and personal sympathy for hitchhikers since Catherine had run out on him two days before. He'd been damn lucky to find the pickup, such as it was, in a section of Campeche where every available vehicle seemed to have a traveling limit of ten kilometers.

The man who'd just climbed in smiled at him and asked in accented Spanish where he was going.

"Chetumal," Jack told him.

"Chetumal is a long way, señor."

"In this baby, it sure is," Jack told him. In his Tracker, on the other hand, Catherine had probably made it by nightfall of the morning she'd left him in her dust. Their friend in the white convertible would have had a little slower time of it, however. Catherine had abandoned his distributor cap at the front desk of the cantina, but while he'd been retrieving it, Jack had made a slight adjustment to his fuel line.

"You have a home in Chetumal?" the passenger asked him over the unsteady roar of the accelerating engine.

"No. A woman."

The passenger glanced at him, nodded, then, with respect asked, "She waits for you there?"

Jack made a noncommittal sound and let the question pass. He'd been letting that question pass since he took off after her. It didn't seem to matter that six times an hour he'd told himself that she was probably better off without him.

That logic couldn't hold a candle to the compulsion that had driven him halfway across Campeche after her.

The truth was that two days of chasing her in this miserable excuse for a pickup had left him with a stubble of beard, a surplus of brooding time, and an attitude that would have rivaled Archie's. He didn't care if she was better off without him. He wanted her anyway. In his bed. In his bar. In his computer files.

"This woman," Jack's passenger commented, "has a special relationship to you?"

"Yeah." Jack grinned wryly at the man. "She stole my truck."

The man glanced over the dashboard, frowning, too polite to comment.

"My other truck," Jack said.

"Ah." The man nodded. "And you intend to get it back."

"I intend," Jack said thoughtfully, "to get satisfaction."

The passenger gave him a look that Jack interpreted as the wary distance of a respectable Mayan when confronted by an unseemly display of machismo on the part of someone less carefully raised.

They drove in silence for ten minutes, then the passenger indicated his stop. Jack pulled over to let him out. The man paused for a moment, his hand on the open window of the door, then offered in parting, "You should remember, Señor, that if you take matters into your own hands in the case of this woman you go after, you will bring yourself trouble."

Jack nodded courteously. "Oh, yes. I know that," he said.

He didn't add that he was going to do it anyway. Avoiding trouble was no longer his priority in this situation.

As a matter of fact, he'd decided, trying to keep Catherine out of trouble and sheltered from turbulence had been one of the dumbest things he'd ever done. She wasn't a woman meant for quiet backwaters. She was meant for brisk winds and turbulent seas.

He recognized the type.

He was just like her.

The music—a blend of marimba and calypso that could have occurred only in Chetumal—was compelling enough to set a mood. The *cerveza* was cold and wet and potent. The business being conducted was varied enough to defy most international laws. But Catherine wasn't drinking, listening, or conducting business.

She was there looking for a man.

She'd been there for the past three nights,

which in La Stela was long enough to give her a regular place at the bar, with the bartender periodically refilling her glass and the regular patrons making a point of knowing her interests.

"Señorita."

She glanced over her shoulder to see Ace making his way toward her. He'd insisted on coming with her to La Stela every night since she'd been back, to watch out for her until his mentor returned. "Over there," he mouthed, gesturing with one shoulder before he turned and melted into the milling crowd.

Jack was standing just inside the door in his leather jacket and what looked to be the same dusty jeans he'd had on when she'd seen him last. His blond hair had fallen over his forehead, his blue eyes were deeply shadowed, and he was slouched against the wall in a way that said *impatience* as clearly as if he'd drawled it into her ear.

Her heart skipped a beat, and her throat went as dry as if she hadn't had any ginger ale for three days.

Their eyes met across the room, and Catherine felt that shock of electricity like a few thousand volts of the real thing.

He wasn't there to apologize. She knew

that as soon as she saw him. He apologized only when he felt like it.

So did she, she realized in an instant. She apologized only when she felt like it too. And what she was feeling at the moment didn't bear the slightest resemblance to an apology.

He walked directly toward her, giving only a passing nod to a few patrons who spoke to him, then leaned into the space beside her at the bar, his hip propped against the brass railing, his gaze taking in her waist-knotted T-shirt and suede skirt. His mouth quirked up at one corner, slowly, then widened into a full smile. "*Hola, querida.*"

She stared at him for a few moments before finally finding her own voice. "Jack. What are you doing here?"

"What do you mean, what am I doing here?" The blue eyes regarded her steadily, levelly, with smoldering masculine implications that raised her blood pressure along with her heartbeat. "You stole my truck."

Catherine sat up a little straighter, facing him on his own level, meeting him stare for stare in this suddenly charged battle of wills. "I did not steal your truck. I borrowed it."

"You *borrowed* it? Lady, you left me stranded in Taxticán with a known criminal!"

"If you were stranded, then how did you get here?"

"You really want to know?"

No, she decided, she didn't think she did. What she wanted to know was far more elemental than the physical details of how they'd gotten to be there, together, standing side by side at the bar, facing each other.

She fished the keys to the Tracker out of her pocket and slapped them on the bar.

He didn't even look at them.

"Your keys," she said helpfully.

He reached for them slowly, then picked them up and closed his fist around them. "All right, lady. Let's go."

"What are you talking about? Go where?"

"I'm taking you home." He pushed away from the bar, gazed at her with blue eyes that had suddenly gone mild and reasonable, and dangled the keys in front of her. "You obviously need a ride, since you just gave away the keys to your transportation."

"I'll get a cab," she told him.

"No."

"Yes!"

"I didn't drive all the way from Taxticán in a 1937 Ford pickup to argue with you, *querida*."

She hadn't waited for him for three nights to argue with him either. She tossed her head back and drew in a deep breath. "What *did* you come for, then?"

"An interesting question."

The soft, cultivated voice intruded on them with no warning. Both of them turned toward the tall, dark man behind them with identical frowns of surprise.

"Mr. Blasquo," Jack said first.

Catherine's eyes widened. Dark hair cut short, standard T-shirt and jeans, a boyish face that surely couldn't have belonged to a criminal, could it?

"An even more interesting question is why he left in the first place. Not to mention you, Señorita." He grinned at her. "But we wouldn't want to leave you out of the equation, would we?"

Jack spoke into the taut silence in a voice pitched low enough so that only the three of them could hear him, but something in the tone of it sent an icy shiver down Catherine's spine.

"I'd *recommend* that you leave her out of it, Blasquo."

"Well." The grin faded, and one dark eyebrow rose. "I didn't think there was any real way to get to you, Gibraltar. I'm glad to know I was wrong."

Catherine's eyes widened. She realized she had suddenly become a pawn in a deadly game, with no warning beyond a seemingly casual greeting from a man she would have been willing to do business with a week earlier.

"Touch her and you'll know how wrong," Jack said. The steadily spoken words left absolutely no room for misinterpretation. This was no con. Catherine knew beyond a shadow of a doubt he meant what he said. She prayed that the man facing him knew it too. She didn't want to see it proven.

"I think you're not seeing the situation correctly, my friend," Blasquo told him, a smile plastered on his face. "According to my sources, the lady is looking for me. I'm just here to oblige."

"You're mistaken," Jack told him. "Wrong message."

"I don't think so." He turned toward Catherine, and she could feel Jack tense. "All I need from you, Catherine, are a few candid answers about your aunt. Nothing too onerous."

"Answers?" Her voice squeaked, but she

let out a quick breath and got it under control. "Oh, I don't have any answers, Mr. Blasquo. I just have questions. I was hoping *you* could give me some answers." She batted her eyelashes at him and gave a helpless, feminine little shrug. "This is all so *mysterious*, I must say."

Blasquo's face lost some of its boyish charm when his mouth hardened and his gaze iced over. "Come now, Catherine. I'm sure we can reach some sort of agreement."

He leaned toward her, lifted his hand, and reached out to touch her hair.

Jack moved so quickly, she couldn't follow what happened. She only knew that seconds later Jack had Blasquo pinned against the bar, his arm twisted behind him, his boyish face grimacing in pain.

"What," Blasquo ground out through his teeth, "do you think you're doing?"

"We're coming to *some sort of agreement*, pal." He tightened his fingers in a seemingly casual gesture, and Blasquo gasped in pain. "I want you to understand just what the consequences are if you ever touch her again."

At the far end of the bar, the bartender glanced toward them warily, but made no move to interfere. The other patrons' reactions didn't go beyond quickly averted glances.

Catherine stared from Blasquo to Jack, her heart pounding with fear.

"And what's in it for me?" Blasquo asked.

For a few seconds the world faded and Catherine was aware only of Jack's dark blue gaze as it locked onto hers and seemed to probe all the way into her soul. Then Jack backed up half a step and eased off infinitesimally on his grip around Blasquo's wrist.

"You'll get what you want, Blasquo. I'm not fool enough to think you'd settle for nothing. But you leave Catherine out of this deal, you understand?"

"Agreed," Blasquo muttered.

Jack glanced up at her again. "Tell him."

"*What?*"

"Tell him, dammit. Everything."

"But . . ." She couldn't believe what he was saying. *Tell Blasquo everything?* Give up on the sting operation he and Madrid had so meticulously constructed?

"The operation's over, Cathy. Trust me."

Trust him?

The blue eyes that were capable of twisting her emotions inside out gazed back at her, unwavering, serious, and with a kind of gravity she found eminently trustworthy.

"The truth," Jack said softly. "Go ahead."

She took a deep breath and started talking.

The story was relatively simple, she found as she said it. Madrid had never believed the codex was a fake. When Blasquo had announced that it was a forgery, Jack had gone public with corroborating evidence so that Blasquo couldn't sell the artifact in any black-market deal until he'd convinced a buyer it was authentic after all.

Jack let up on Blasquo's arm, and the man pushed himself up from the bar, wincing as he massaged his wrenched shoulder. "The codex, then, in your opinion, is authentic," he said to Jack. His voice was strained, but there was a glint of triumph in his face that revolted Catherine. Jack said nothing.

"Your opinion, of course, is wrong," Blasquo announced. "Madrid will find no evidence to the contrary. I think she will realize it's necessary to return home immediately."

"No doubt," Jack muttered.

Blasquo was enjoying this, Catherine realized, though he was keeping his distance from Jack. A wrenched arm was apparently a small price to pay for the pleasure of discovering he could turn a profit on his country's heritage.

"I trust you will give her that message," Blasquo went on.

"She'll get it."

He glanced toward Catherine again, then, with a sideways glance toward Jack, and keeping his hands carefully on the bar, he leaned toward her and murmured, "A shame you didn't contact me earlier, Catherine. You might have had a chance to see the disputed codex. Who knows what you might have found out about its authenticity?"

He turned, smiled maliciously at Jack, then made his way out of the bar, his hand cradling his shoulder but his posture insolent.

Jack watched him out, his face set and impassive, then turned back to Catherine.

There was a blaze of anger in his eyes that broke through her numbness like a hot knife through butter.

"What?" she said, startled.

"You! What the hell were you doing hanging out here waiting for that scum?"

"I just wanted to talk to him."

"*Talk* to him? Talk to him! Didn't it occur to you that could be dangerous? And that line about not knowing anything—dammit, Cathy, what the hell did you think you were doing?"

"I was trying to protect your operation!"

He swore, imaginatively, in two languages.

"Well, don't get hysterical about it," she snapped.

"*Hysterical?* You want to see hysterical, you just try something like that again, you hear me?"

"Me? What about you threatening to break his arm. What if he'd gotten the jump on you and twisted *your* arm? He probably would have broken it!"

"Not a chance, Cath. Not after he tried to touch you."

Her gathering outrage evaporated, stopped short by his response. Her heart skipped, her throat tightened.

Hope flared inside her along with a sudden vivid picture of what she wanted. What she hoped for. Afraid to test it, she looked away from him, her hands gripping the edge of the bar nervously.

"Do you really think the sting is over, especially now that Blasquo knows everything?" she asked him.

He didn't answer her. Finally curious enough to risk it, she looked up at him.

"Forget the sting, Cathy. I've got a question for you."

"What?"

He opened his mouth, then shut it again and closed his eyes. "It's not a question," he said. "It's a statement. About you and me. About you. About . . . how I feel about you."

Catherine felt something light and fizzy racing through her veins, making her dizzy.

"Which I have a hard time saying, *querida*."

"Maybe . . . you could . . . show me."

"I already did. In Taxticán. At the site, in the jungle. That was showing you, Cath. That wasn't any con."

Suddenly there didn't seem to be enough oxygen in the room, and Catherine felt her lungs burning. She stood there, transfixed by his admission, unable to make any sound.

Jack ran his fingers through his hair, raking it back from his face. It fell forward again as soon as he dropped his hand. His face looked gaunt. He hadn't shaved in days, she realized. He must have been on the road, driving straight through from Taxticán. His jeans were dusty, his T-shirt obviously fresh out of the duffel bag. Even his leather jacket was wrinkled. She'd never seen a man she wanted more.

She tried to tell him so, but the words couldn't get past the lump in her throat. She could do no more than raise her eyes to meet his.

"Oh, babe," he said. He took a step closer to her, and she watched as his hand reached out to touch her hair, brush it back over her shoulder. "I want to say this right this time," he murmured. "I don't want you to think—" He raked his hand through his hair again. "I don't want you to walk away this time, Cathy."

"I'm not walking," she whispered, finally finding her voice.

He took the last step toward her, cupped his hands around her face, and pulled her close. "*Estoy enamorado contigo, querida.*"

She wrapped her arms around his waist, absorbing the closeness of him, the sheer joy of having him with her.

"I think I have been ever since I followed you to Taxticán. When I saw you there, in the jungle, with your Jeep half in that trench, I knew I didn't want to let you go."

"You said it was just a con game, Jack. A cover story. I had to prove I could carry it off."

His mouth curved in a slight, tentative smile that made her heart turn over. "The only one I was conning was me," he said softly. "I just needed time to make sure you wouldn't want to go, Cathy. I was afraid you'd just walk out of my life and never look back. And I was afraid of how I was going to feel when you did."

"And then I did," she said, regret in her voice.

"And I was right," he went on. "Dammit, Cath, I felt just like Archie."

"Archie?"

He threaded his hands deeper into her hair. "I want you to meet Archie, Cath. As a matter of fact, I want—" He lifted his head far enough to lock her gaze onto his. "Cathy," he said, "I have a one bedroom apartment in Chetumal with a landlady who speaks only Mayan when the plumbing goes on the fritz. I talk to a lizard. A gang of juvenile delinquents like Ace drop in at all hours of the day and night, and my career hit bottom about five minutes ago. So how about it, Cath—will you marry me?"

She stared at him while a wave of pure joy hit her broadside.

"I don't think I can keep you out of trouble, Cathy," he said, "but I want to be there when you get into it, beside you, helping you get out of it . . . or stay in it, whatever the hell you want, wherever you want."

"Yes," she told him. "Yes. Yes. *Sí*. I will."

"You will?"

"I'm in love with you too, Jack. In Spanish, in English, whatever language you want."

"Oh, Cathy . . ." He brought his mouth closer to hers. "As soon as I get another job, as soon as this Blasquo deal gets squared away, will you marry me?"

She let him kiss her because she couldn't resist the temptation, then she said against his mouth, "Actually, Jack . . . about Blasquo . . ."

"Hmm?" he murmured.

"Maybe it will be squared away if my aunt has just a little evidence. Blasquo *did* intimate that the codex was authentic."

Reluctantly, he stopped kissing her and raised his head to look at her again. Then he told her about his conversation with Madrid.

"Why didn't you let me know sooner?" she asked. "Then I wouldn't have bothered to tape Blasquo."

"Tape?"

She nodded. "In my purse. I had the volume turned all the way up."

Jack glanced down at the purse she had propped on the bar beside her elbow. Catherine reached into it and pulled out the tape recorder, still running. Jack was looking at her with a mixture of disbelief, outrage, and something she could describe only as awe.

She pressed the rewind button for a few seconds, then played the tape back.

Jack's voice, muffled but clearly audible, said, " . . . about it, Cath. Will you marry me?"

His wide mouth spread in a grin that lit up Catherine's soul. "Oh, babe," he said, shaking his head, "no one has ever recorded me proposing marriage before this."

"It will probably be played in court," she said, teasing him. "At the hearing involving Blasquo."

"That's okay with me, Cath. As long as they also play back the part about you saying yes."

She pulled him a little bit closer. "Ask me back to your apartment, and I'll say it again."

He turned her toward the door, picked up her purse for her, and started walking her through the crowd of patrons who, now that the potential danger was over, glanced toward them with open curiosity and knowing smiles.

"Save that answer," Jack told her. "I've got another question I'll want it for."

"What?"

"I'll ask you later, *querida*," he said. "In Spanish."

THE EDITOR'S CORNER

Since the inception of LOVESWEPT in 1983, we've been known as the most innovative publisher of category romance. We were the first to publish authors under their real names and show their photographs in the books. We originated interconnected "series" books and established theme months. And now, after publishing over 700 books, we are once again changing the face of category romance.

Starting next month, we are introducing a brand-new LOVESWEPT look. We're sure you'll agree with us that it's distinctive and outstanding—nothing less than the perfect showcase for your favorite authors and the wonderful stories they write.

A second change is that we are now publishing four LOVESWEPTs a month instead of six. With so many romances on the market today, we want to provide you with only the very best in romantic fiction. We know that you want quality, not quantity, and we are as committed as ever to giving you love stories you'll never forget, by authors you'll always remember. We are especially proud to debut our new look with four sizzling romances from four of our most talented authors.

Starting off our new look is Mary Kay McComas with **WAIT FOR ME**, LOVESWEPT #702. Oliver Carey saves Holly Loftin's life during an earthquake with a split-second tackle, but only when their eyes meet does he feel the earth tremble and her compassionate soul reach out to his. He is intrigued by her need to help others, enchanted by her appetite for simple pleasures, but now he has to show her that their differences can be their strengths and that, more than anything, they belong together. Mary Kay will have you laughing and crying with this touching romance.

The ever-popular Kay Hooper is back with her unique blend of romantic mystery and spicy wit in **THE HAUNTING OF JOSIE**, LOVESWEPT #703. Josie Douglas decides that Marc Westbrook, her gorgeous landlord, would have made a good warlock, with his raven-dark hair, silver eyes, and even a black cat in his arms! She chose the isolated house as a refuge, a place to put the past to rest, but now Marc insists on fighting her demons . . . and why does he so resemble the ghostly figure who beckons to her from the head of the stairs? Kay once more demonstrates her talent for seduction and suspense in this wonderful romance.

Theresa Gladden proves that opposites attract in **PERFECT TIMING**, LOVESWEPT #704. Jenny Johnson isn't looking for a new husband, no matter how many hunks her sister sends her way, but Carter Dalton's cobalt-blue eyes mesmerize her into letting his daughter join her girls' club—and inviting him to dinner! The free-spirited rebel is all wrong for him: messy house, too many pets, wildly disorganized—but he can't resist a woman who promises to fill the empty spaces he didn't know he had. Theresa's spectacular romance will leave you breathless.

Last but certainly not least is **TAMING THE PIRATE**, LOVESWEPT #705, from the supertalented Ruth Owen. When investigator Gabe Ramirez sees Laurie Palmer, she stirs to life the appetites of his buccaneer ancestors and makes him long for the golden lure of her smile. She longs to trade her secrets for one kiss from his brigand's lips, but once he knows why she is on the run, will he betray the woman he's vowed will never escape his arms? You won't forget this wonderful story from Ruth.

Happy reading,

With warmest wishes,

Nita Taublib

Nita Taublib

Deputy Publisher

P.S. Don't miss the exciting women's novels from Bantam that are coming your way in August—**MIDNIGHT WARRIOR**, by *New York Times* bestselling author Iris Johansen, is a spellbinding tale of pursuit, possession, and passion that extends from the wilds of Normandy to untamed medieval England; **BLUE MOON** is a powerful and romantic novel of love and families by the exceptionally talented Luanne Rice. *The New York Times Book Review* calls it "a rare combination of realism and romance"; **VELVET**, by Jane Feather, is a spectacular novel of danger and deception in which a beautiful woman risks all for revenge and love; **THE WITCH DANCE**, by Peggy Webb, is a poignant story of two lovers whose passion breaks every rule. We'll be giving you a sneak peek at these terrific books in next month's LOVESWEPTs. And immediately following this page, look for a preview of the exciting romances from Bantam that are *available now!*

"Power, passion, tragedy, and triumph are Rosanne Bittner's hallmarks. Again and again, she brings readers to tears."
—*Romantic Times*

WILDEST DREAMS

by

ROSANNE BITTNER

Against the glorious panorama of big sky country, award-winning Rosanne Bittner creates a sweeping saga of passion, excitement, and danger . . . as a beautiful young woman and a rugged ex-soldier struggle against all odds to carve out an empire—and to forge a magnificent love.

Here is a look at this powerful novel . . .

Lettie walked ahead of him into the shack, swallowing back an urge to retch. She gazed around the cabin, noticed a few cracks between the boards that were sure to let in cold drafts in the winter. A rat scurried across the floor, and she stepped back. The room was very small, perhaps fifteen feet square, with a potbellied stove in one corner, a few shelves built against one wall, and a crudely built table in the middle of the room, with two crates to serve as chairs. The bed was made from pine, with ropes for springs and no mattress on top. She was glad her mother had given her two feather mattresses before they parted. Never had she longed more fervently to be with her family back at the spacious home they had left behind in St.

Joseph, where people lived in reasonable numbers, and anything they needed was close at hand.

Silently, she untied and removed the wool hat she'd been wearing. She was shaken by her sense of doubt, not only over her choice to come to this lonely, desolate place, but also over her decision to marry. She loved Luke, and he had been attentive and caring and protective throughout their dangerous, trying journey to get here; but being his wife meant fulfilling other needs he had not yet demanded of her. This was the very first time they had been truly alone since marrying at Fort Laramie. When Luke had slept in the wagon with her, he had only held her. Was he waiting for her to make the first move; or had he patiently been waiting for this moment, when he had her alone? Between the realization that he would surely expect to consummate their marriage now, and the knowledge that she would spend the rest of the winter holed up in this tiny cabin, with rats running over her feet, she felt panic building.

"Lettie?"

She was startled by the touch of Luke's hand on her shoulder. She gasped and turned to look up at him, her eyes wide with fear and apprehension. "I . . . I don't know if I can stay here, Luke." Oh, why had she said that? She could see the hurt in his eyes. He should be angry. Maybe he would throw her down and have his way with her now, order her to submit to her husband, yell at her for being weak and selfish, tell her she would stay here whether she liked it or not.

He turned, looked around the tiny room, looked back at her with a smile of resignation on his face. "I can't blame you there. I don't know why I even considered this. I guess in all my excitement . . ." He sighed deeply. "I'll take you back to Billings in the morning. It's not much of a town, but maybe I can find a safe place for you and Nathan to stay while I make things more livable around here."

"But . . . you'd be out here all alone."

He shrugged, walking over to the stove and opening the door. "I knew before I ever came here there would be a lot of lonely living I'd have to put up with." He picked up some kindling from a small pile that lay near the stove and stacked it inside. "When you have a dream, you simply do what you have to do to realize it." He turned to face her. "I told you it won't be like this forever, Lettie, and it won't."

His eyes moved over her, and she knew what he wanted. He simply loved and respected her too much to ask for it. A wave of guilt rushed through her, and she felt like crying. "I'm sorry, Luke. I've disappointed you in so many ways already."

He frowned, coming closer. "I never said that. I don't blame you for not wanting to stay here. I'll take you back to town and you can come back here in the spring." He placed his hands on her shoulders. "I love you, Lettie. I never want you to be unhappy or wish you had never married me. I made you some promises, and I intend to keep them."

A lump seemed to rise in her throat. "You'd really take me to Billings? You wouldn't be angry about it?"

Luke studied her face. He wanted her so, but was not sure how to approach the situation because of what she had been through. He knew there was a part of her that wanted him that way, but he had not seen it in her eyes since leaving Fort Laramie. He had only seen doubt and fear. "I told you I'd take you. I wouldn't be angry."

She suddenly smiled, although there were tears in her eyes. "That's all I need to know. I . . . I thought you took it for granted, just because I was your wife . . . that you'd demand . . ."

She threw her arms around him, resting her face against his thick fur jacket. "Oh, Luke, forgive me. You don't have to take me back. As long as I know I *can* go back, that's all I need to know. Does that make any sense?"

He grinned. "I think so."

Somewhere in the distance they heard the cry of a bobcat. Combined with the groaning mountain wind, the sounds only accentuated how alone they really were, a good five miles from the only town, and no sign of civilization for hundreds of miles beyond that. "I can't let you stay out here alone. You're my husband. I belong here with you," Lettie said, still clinging to him.

Luke kissed her hair, her cheek. She found herself turning to meet his lips, and he explored her mouth savagely then. She felt lost in his powerful hold, buried in the fur jacket, suddenly weak. How well he fit this land, so tall and strong and rugged and determined. She loved him all the more for it.

He left her mouth, kissed her neck. "I'd better get a fire going, bring in—"

"Luke." She felt her heart racing as all her fears began to melt away. She didn't know how to tell him, what to do. She could only look into those handsome blue eyes and say his name. She met his lips again, astonished at the sudden hunger in her soul. How could she have considered letting this poor man stay out here alone, when he had a wife and child who could help him, love him? And how could she keep denying him the one thing he had every right to take for himself? Most of all, how could she deny her own sudden desires, this surprising awakening of woman that ached to be set free?

"Luke," she whispered. "I want to be your wife, Luke, in every way. I want to be one with you and know that it's all right. I don't want to be afraid any more."

DANGEROUS TO LOVE

by Elizabeth Thornton

"A major, major talent . . . a genre superstar."
—*Rave Reviews*

Dangerous. Wild. Reckless. Those were the words that passed through Serena Ward's mind the moment Julian Raynor entered the gaming hall. If anyone could penetrate Serena's disguise—and jeopardize the political fugitives she was delivering to freedom—surely it would be London's most notorious gamester. Yet when the militia storms the establishment in search of traitors, Raynor provides just the pretext Serena needs to escape. But Serena is playing with fire . . . and before the night is through she will find herself surrendering to the heat of unsuspected desires.

The following is a sneak preview of what transpires that evening in a private room above the gaming hall. . .

"Let's start over, shall we?" said Julian. He returned to the chair he had vacated. "And this time, I shall try to keep myself well in check. No, don't move. I rather like you kneeling at my feet in an attitude of submission."

He raised his wine glass and imbibed slowly. "Now you," he said. When she made to take it from him, he shook his head. "No, I shall hold it. Come closer."

Once again she found herself between his thighs. She didn't know what to do with her hands, but he knew.

"Place them on my thighs," he said, and Serena obeyed. Beneath her fingers, she could feel the hard masculine muscles bunch and strain. She was also acutely aware of the movements of the militia as they combed the building for Jacobites.

"Drink," he said, holding the rim of the glass to her lips, tipping it slightly.

Wine flooded her mouth and spilled over. Choking, she swallowed it.

"Allow me," he murmured. As one hand cupped her neck, his head descended and his tongue plunged into her mouth.

Shock held her rigid as his tongue thrust, and thrust again, circling, licking at the dregs of wine in her mouth, lapping it up with avid enjoyment. When she began to struggle, his powerful thighs tightened against her, holding her effortlessly. Her hands went to his chest to push him away, and slipped between the parted edges of his shirt. Warm masculine flesh quivered beneath the pads of her fingertips. Splaying her hands wide, with every ounce of strength, she shoved at him, trying to free herself.

He released her so abruptly that she tumbled to the floor. Scrambling away from him, she came up on her knees. They were both breathing heavily.

Frowning, he rose to his feet and came to tower over her. "What game are you playing now?"

"No game," she quickly got out. "You are going too fast for me." She carefully rose to her feet and began to inch away from him. "We have yet to settle on my . . . my remuneration."

"Remuneration?" He laughed softly. "Sweetheart, I have already made up my mind that for a woman of your unquestionable talents, no price is too high."

These were not the words that Serena wanted to hear, nor did she believe him. Men did not like greedy women. Although she wasn't supposed to know it, long before his marriage, her brother, Jeremy, had given his mistress her *congé* because the girl was too demanding. What was it the girl had wanted?

Her back came up against the door to the bedchamber. One hand curved around the door-knob in a reflexive movement, the other clutched the door-jamb for support.

Licking her lips, she said, "I . . . I shall want my own house."

He cocked his head to one side. As though musing to himself, he said, "I've never had a woman in my keeping. Do you know, for the first time, I can see the merit in it? Fine, you shall have your house."

He took a step closer, and she flattened herself against the door. "And . . . and my own carriage?" She could hardly breathe with him standing so close to her.

"Done." His eyes were glittering.

When he lunged for her, she cried out and flung herself into the bed-chamber, slamming the door quickly, bracing her shoulder against it as her fingers fumbled for the key.

One kick sent both door and Serena hurtling back. He stood framed in the doorway, the light behind him, and every sensible thought went out of her head. Dangerous. Reckless. Wild. This was all a game to him!

He feinted to the left, and she made a dash for the door, twisting away as his hands reached for her. His fingers caught on the back of her gown, ripping it to the waist. One hand curved around her arm, sending her sprawling against the bed.

There was no candle in the bed-chamber, but the lights from the tavern's courtyard filtered through the window casting a luminous glow. He was shedding the last of his clothes. Although everything in her revolted against it, she knew that the time had come to reveal her name.

Summoning the remnants of her dignity, she said, "You should know that I am no common doxy. I am a high-born lady."

He laughed in that way of his that she was coming to thoroughly detest. "I know," he said, "and I am to play the conqueror. Sweetheart, those games are all very well in their place. But the time for games is over. I want a real woman in my arms tonight, a willing one and not some character from a fantasy."

She turned his words over in her mind and

could make no sense of them. Seriously doubting the man's sanity, she cried out, "Touch me and you will regret it to your dying day. Don't you understand anything? I am a lady. I . . ."

He fell on her and rolled with her on the bed. Subduing her easily with the press of his body, he rose above her. "Have done with your games. I am Julian. You are Victoria. I am your protector. You are my mistress. Yield to me, sweeting."

Bought and paid for—that was what was in his mind. She was aware of something else. He didn't want to hurt or humiliate her. He wanted to have his way with her. He thought he had that right.

He wasn't moving, or forcing his caresses on her. He was simply holding her, watching her with an unfathomable expression. "Julian," she whispered, giving him his name in an attempt to soften him. "Victoria Noble is not my real name."

"I didn't think it was," he said, and kissed her.

His mouth was gentle; his tongue caressing, slipping between her teeth, not deeply, not threateningly, but inviting her to participate in the kiss. For a moment, curiosity held her spellbound. She had never been kissed like this before. It was like sinking into a bath of spiced wine. It was sweet and intoxicating, just like the taste of him.

Shivering, she pulled out of the embrace and stared up at him. His brows were raised, questioning her. All she need do was tell him her name and he would let her go.

Suddenly it was the last thing she wanted to do.

An All-Time Recommended Read in the
Romance Reader's Handbook

AMAZON LILY

by the spectacular

Theresa Weir

"Theresa Weir's writing is poignant, passionate and powerful . . . will capture the hearts of readers."—*New York Times* bestselling author Jayne Ann Krentz

Winner of Romantic Times *New Adventure Writer Award, Theresa Weir captures your heart with this truly irresistible story of two remarkable people who must battle terrifying danger even as they discover breathtaking love.* Rave Reviews *had praised it as "a splendid adventure . . . the perfect way to get away from it all," and* Rendezvous *insists that you "put it on your must-read list."*

"You must be the Lily-Libber who's going to San Reys."

The deep voice that came slicing through Corey's sleep-fogged brain was gravelly and rough-edged.

She dragged open heavy-lidded eyes to find herself contemplating a ragged pair of grubby blue tennis shoes. She allowed her gaze to pan slowly northward, leaving freeze-framed images etched in her mind's eye: long jeans faded to almost white except along the stitching; a copper waistband button with moldy lettering; a large expanse of chest-filled, sweat-soaked T-shirt; a stubbly field of several days growth of whiskers; dark aviator sunglasses that met the dusty, sweaty brim of a New York Yankees baseball cap.

Corey's head was bent back at an uncomfortable angle. Of course, Santarém, Brazil, wasn't Illinois, and this person certainly wasn't like any case she'd ever handled in her job as a social worker.

The squalid air-taxi building was really little more than a shed, and it had been crowded before, with just Corey and the files. But now, with this man in front of her giving off his angry aura . . . She couldn't see his eyes, but she could read enough of his expression to know that she was being regarded as a lower form of life or something he might have scraped off the bottom off his shoe.

She knew she wasn't an American beauty. Her skin was too pale, her brown eyes too large for her small face, giving her a fragile, old-world appearance that was a burden in these modern times. People had a tendency to either overlook her completely or coddle her. But his reaction was something totally new.

The man's attention shifted from her to the smashed red packet in his hand. He pulled out a flattened nonfilter cigarette, smoothed it until it was somewhat round, then stuck it in the corner of his mouth. One hand moved across the front of the faded green T-shirt that clung damply to his corded muscles. He slapped at the breast pocket. Not finding what he was searching for, both of his hands moved to the front pockets of the ancient jeans that covered those long, athletic legs. There was a frayed white horizontal rip across his right knee, tan skin and sun-bleached hair showing through. Change jingled as he rummaged around to finally pull out a damp, wadded-up book of matches.

"Damn," he muttered after the third match failed to light. "Gotta quit sweating so much." He tossed the bedraggled matchbook to the floor. Cigarette still in his mouth, his hands began a repeat search of his pockets.

Corey reached over to where her twill shoulder bag was lying on a stack of tattered *Mad* magazines. She unzipped a side pocket and pulled out the glossy black and gold matches she'd been saving to add to her matchbook collection.

He grabbed them without so much as a thank-you. "That's right—" he said, striking a match, "you girl scouts are always prepared." He shook out the match and tossed it to the floor.

"Are you Mike Jones?" She hoped to God he wasn't the pilot she was waiting for.

"No." He inhaled deeply, then exhaled, blowing a thick cloud of smoke her direction.

"Do you know when Mr. Jones will be here?" she asked, willing her eyes not to bat against the smoke.

"*Mister* Jones had a slight setback. He was unconscious last time I saw him." The man read the ornate advertisement for the Black Tie restaurant on the match cover, then tucked the matches into the breast pocket of his T-shirt. The knuckles of his hand were red and swollen, one finger joint cracked and covered with dried blood.

"I found Jones in a local cantina, drunk out of his mind and just itching to fly. Had a little trouble convincing him it would be in his best interest if he stayed on the ground. My name's Ash—Asher Adams, and it looks like I'll be flying you to the reserve. If you still want to go."

Corey pushed her earlier thoughts to the back of her mind. "Of course I still want to go." She hadn't come this far to back out now.

"You want my advice?" He pulled off the navy-blue cap and swiped at his sweating forehead before slapping the cap back over shaggy brown hair. "Go back home. Get married. Have babies. Why is it you women have to prove you're men? You come here thrill-seeking so you can go home and be some kind of small-town hero. So your whole puny story can be printed up in a little four-page county paper and you can travel around to all the local clubs and organizations with your slide presentation, and all your friends can ooh and aah over you."

Corey felt heated anger flushing her face. She pressed her lips together in a firm, stubborn line.

What an obnoxious boor! In her years as a social worker, she'd never, *never* come across anyone like him. And thank God for that, she fumed.

Asher Adams took another drag off his cigarette, then flopped down in the chair across from her, legs sticking out in front of him, crossed at the ankles. "Go back home," he said in a weary voice. "This is real. It isn't some Humphrey Bogart movie. This isn't Sleepyville, Iowa, or wherever the hell you're from—"

"Pleasant Grove, Illinois," she flatly informed him. "And I don't need your advice. I don't want it." Who did this overbearing man think he was? She hadn't taken vacation time to come here and be insulted by an ill-tempered woman-hater. And he talked as if she planned to settle in the jungles of Brazil. There was nothing further from her mind.

She zipped her bag and grabbed up her cream-colored wool jacket. "I'd like to leave now."

And don't miss these fabulous romances from Bantam Books, on sale in July:

MIDNIGHT WARRIOR

by the *New York Times* bestselling author

Iris Johansen

"Iris Johansen is a master among master stoytellers."

—*Affaire de Coeur*

BLUE MOON

by the nationally bestselling author

Luanne Rice

"Luanne Rice proves herself a nimble virtuoso."

—*The Washington Post Book World*

VELVET

by the highly acclaimed

Jane Feather

"An author to treasure."

—*Romantic Times*

THE WITCH DANCE

by the incomparable

Peggy Webb

"Ms. Webb has an inventive mind brimming with originality that makes all of her books special reading."

—*Romantic Times*

OFFICIAL RULES

To enter the sweepstakes below carefully follow all instructions found elsewhere in this offer.

The **Winners Classic** will award prizes with the following approximate maximum values: 1 Grand Prize: $26,500 (or $25,000 cash alternate); 1 First Prize: $3,000; 5 Second Prizes: $400 each; 35 Third Prizes: $100 each; 1,000 Fourth Prizes: $7.50 each. Total maximum retail value of Winners Classic Sweepstakes is $42,500. Some presentations of this sweepstakes may contain individual entry numbers corresponding to one or more of the aforementioned prize levels. To determine the Winners, individual entry numbers will first be compared with the winning numbers preselected by computer. For winning numbers not returned, prizes will be awarded in random drawings from among all eligible entries received. Prize choices may be offered at various levels. If a winner chooses an automobile prize, all license and registration fees, taxes, destination charges and, other expenses not offered herein are the responsibility of the winner. If a winner chooses a trip, travel must be complete within one year from the time the prize is awarded. Minors must be accompanied by an adult. Travel companion(s) must also sign release of liability. Trips are subject to space and departure availability. Certain black-out dates may apply.

The following applies to the sweepstakes named above:

No purchase necessary. You can also enter the sweepstakes by sending your name and address to: P.O. Box 508, Gibbstown, N.J. 08027. Mail each entry separately. Sweepstakes begins 6/1/93. Entries must be received by 12/30/94. Not responsible for lost, late, damaged, misdirected, illegible or postage due mail. Mechanically reproduced entries are not eligible. All entries become property of the sponsor and will not be returned.

Prize Selection/Validations: Selection of winners will be conducted no later than 5:00 PM on January 28, 1995, by an independent judging organization whose decisions are final. Random drawings will be held at 1211 Avenue of the Americas, New York, N.Y. 10036. Entrants need not be present to win. Odds of winning are determined by total number of entries received. Circulation of this sweepstakes is estimated not to exceed 200 million. All prizes are guaranteed to be awarded and delivered to winners. Winners will be notified by mail and may be required to complete an affidavit of eligibility and release of liability which must be returned within 14 days of date on notification or alternate winners will be selected in a random drawing. Any prize notification letter or any prize returned to a participating sponsor, Bantam Doubleday Dell Publishing Group, Inc., its participating divisions or subsidiaries, or the independent judging organization as undeliverable will be awarded to an alternate winner. Prizes are not transferable. No substitution for prizes except as offered or as may be necessary due to unavailability, in which case a prize of equal or greater value will be awarded. Prizes will be awarded approximately 90 days after the drawing. All taxes are the sole responsibility of the winners. Entry constitutes permission (except where prohibited by law) to use winners' names, hometowns, and likenesses for publicity purposes without further or other compensation. Prizes won by minors will be awarded in the name of parent or legal guardian.

Participation: Sweepstakes open to residents of the United States and Canada, except for the province of Quebec. Sweepstakes sponsored by Bantam Doubleday Dell Publishing Group, Inc., (BDD), 1540 Broadway, New York, NY 10036. Versions of this sweepstakes with different graphics and prize choices will be offered in conjunction with various solicitations or promotions by different subsidiaries and divisions of BDD. Where applicable, winners will have their choice of any prize offered at level won. Employees of BDD, its divisions, subsidiaries, advertising agencies, independent judging organization, and their immediate family members are not eligible.

Canadian residents, in order to win, must first correctly answer a time limited arithmetical skill testing question. Void in Puerto Rico, Quebec and wherever prohibited or restricted by law. Subject to all federal, state, local and provincial laws and regulations. For a list of major prize winners (available after 1/29/95): send a self-addressed, stamped envelope entirely separate from your entry to: Sweepstakes Winners, P.O. Box 517, Gibbstown, NJ 08027. Requests must be received by 12/30/94. DO NOT SEND ANY OTHER CORRESPONDENCE TO THIS P.O. BOX.

SWP 7/93